In wild haste now, Tyeema spun on his heel to face Captain Macready, both hands clubbed around the empty musket. But Musketabah, as he had hoped, had leaped with his expected quickness. Sitting on the ground quite close to the captain, he had simply lunged sideways and yanked the white man's feet from under him, then grappled him.

Musketabah had a death grip on the man. Musketabah brought Macready's rifle across the white man's throat, and pressed down on his windpipe, crushing it. Captain Macready's mouth sagged open, but he was still fumbling along his belt for his hunting knife. Tyeema got there first, pulled the knife from its sheath, and plunged it into the militia captain's heart.

Musketabah rolled the dead man aside and got to his feet. The others would be coming fast; the musket shot would bring them, Tyeema pointed out, and there was no time to lose....

Other *Leisure* Double Westerns by T.V. Olsen:
**GUNSWIFT/RAMROD RIDER
THE MAN FROM NOWHERE/BITTER GRASS
A MAN CALLED BRAZOS/BRAND OF THE STAR
McGIVERN/THE HARD MEN
CANYON OF THE GUN/
    HAVEN OF THE HUNTED
HIGH LAWLESS/SAVAGE SIERRA**

Western Sagas:
**ARROW IN THE SUN
RED IS THE RIVER
THERE WAS A SEASON**

WESTWARD THEY RODE

T. V. OLSEN

LEISURE BOOKS   NEW YORK CITY

ACKNOWLEDGMENTS

BACKTRAIL © 1956 by Best Books, Inc. Revised from version in *Ranch Romances* (April 6, 1956).

THE CACHE AND THE CONVICT © 1956 by Best Books, Inc. Revised from version in *Ranch Romances* (August 24, 1956).

A KIND OF COURAGE © 1970 by Western Writers of America, Inc. Reprinted from WITH GUIDONS FLYING edited by Charles N. Heckelmann (Doubleday, 1970).

THE STRANGE VALLEY © 1968 by T.V. Olsen. Reprinted from GREAT GHOST STORIES OF THE OLD WEST edited by Betty Baker (Four Winds, 1968).

THE RECKONING © 1975 by Avenue Victor Hugo, Inc. Reprinted from *Fiction* (Number 9, 1975).

THE WAR AT PEACEVILLE © 1956 by Best Books, Inc. Revised from version in *Ranch Romances* (September 7, 1956).

NO-FIGHTS © 1968 by T.V. Olsen. Reprinted from WAR WHOOP AND BATTLE CRY edited by Brian Garfield (Scholastic, 1968).

THEY WALKED TALL © 1963 by T.V. Olsen. Reprinted from PICK OF THE ROUNDUP edited by Stephen Payne (Avon, 1963).

A LEISURE BOOK®

June 1996

Published by special arrangement with
Golden West Literary Agency.

Dorchester Publishing Co., Inc.
276 Fifth Avenue
New York, NY 10001

If you purchased this book without a cover you should be aware that this book is stolen property. It was reported as "unsold and destroyed" to the publisher and neither the author nor the publisher has received any payment for this "stripped book."

Copyright © 1976 by T.V. Olsen

All rights reserved. No part of this book may be reproduced or transmitted in any form or by any electronic or mechanical means, including photocopying, recording or by any information storage and retrieval system, without the written permission of the Publisher, except where permitted by law.

The name "Leisure Books" and the stylized "L" with design are trademarks of Dorchester Publishing Co., Inc.

Printed in the United States of America.

WESTWARD THEY RODE

BACKTRAIL

The sun was climbing toward mid-morning as John Fallon pulled his spring wagon up beside a half-dozen other rigs in the empty lot by the Crane's Crossing frame courthouse. Fallon unhitched the horses, watered them, and tied them at the long hitch rack. Afterward he glanced at the Stockman's Saloon across the street, then walked back to the wagon and gave his wife a half-absent grin.

"Let's get to that shopping, Ef——" He swung her down from the high seat.

Effie smiled faintly. A healthy, pale-haired woman, she had a way of anticipating him that he did not find unpleasant.

"What am I, your wife or your keeper? Get over to the saloon and have your drink with your cronies. You can meet me at the store later."

"I can, can't I?" Fallon started across the street, paused halfway, and glanced over his shoulder. "By the way, I'm low on tobacco—"

"I won't forget. Go on, you're thirsty."

He walked on, a big, still-faced man in his late twenties whose Indian-dark hair was already gray-streaked, who wore rough trousers, hickory shirt, and a farmer's thick-soled work shoes.

An early coolness still clung to the stale interior of the Stockman's. The room was long and high-ceilinged, the bar curving out from an opening by the door and running the length of the room to the rear wall. A number of men, not unusual on a Saturday morning, were at the bar, talking more than drinking, out of deference to their wives and the early hour.

Experience had keened Fallon to gauge the moods of men quickly and correctly. There had been other times, other places, when simple survival had hinged on his ability to assess men quickly. He felt an uneasy current running through the low talk as he moved to the bar, greeting men he knew with a word or nod. Even his friend, stout Tom Claussen, who owned a place south of his, gave only a bare and morose response to his greeting.

Fallon signaled Benny behind the bar for whiskey, then came to stand by old March Beckworth and his nineteen-year-old son, Hugo.

"Morning, John."

"Howdy, March. Hugo—"

The Beckworths farmed a quarter section adjoining Fallon's. Old March was a huge, weatherworn man with pleasant eyes that had found life good. He'd been the first homesteader to enter this Wyoming valley, and his word and opinion carried weight with his neighbors.

"Hah-yuh," said Hugo Beckworth. He was a tall, gangling, wire-tempered youth who never stood quite still. He twitched and foot-shifted, lightly drumming his glass on the bar. His pale, shallow eyes held little promise of his father's strength, but Fallon knew a man could never be sure of a colt till it had its full legs under it. The only sure measure of Hugo was he had some tall growing to do yet.

Fallon lifted his drink and tossed it down, letting its heat curl around his belly before saying idly, "Tom dropped by last evening. Been out at your place, he said."

"Well then," March Beckworth said dryly, "I don't need to tell you Kane Eldridge paid a call while Tom was there." His big resonant voice held an edge that Fallon didn't miss.

"Gave you a sort of hoorawing, Claussen said."

"I'd say that's about right. Eldridge, he brought along his foreman, Dixon, and that new man of his, huh, what's his name—"

"Lomax, Pa," said Hugo. "Jeez."

"Frankie Lomax," Fallon said quietly.

"That's right. Well, Eldridge, he claimed a half-dozen of his prime yearlings ranging over by my line was missing. One word led to another and pretty soon he made bold to accuse me of killing the animals for meat. Said if it happens again, he will be back with his whole damn crew and we will try conclusions."

"He has made talk before."

"Not like this. This was war talk, John. He means it, I'm thinking."

Several nearby drinkers had taken notice of the conversation and had broken off their talk, listening to Fallon and Beckworth. They had cause to.

Kane Eldridge, who owned the sprawling Wineglass ranch, was a cattleman of an old, earthy breed who had fought hard for the open range he claimed. He'd vowed off and on to put the run on every damned sodman in the valley, many of whom looked more or less to March Beckworth to guide their own behavior. With this reliance, unspoken though it was, ran a considerable feeling that if March Beckworth couldn't hold on, neither could anyone else.

"I tried to reason with the man," March said. "But . . ." He let his massive stooped shoulders lift and fall in a shrug.

A hot glint touched young Hugo's eyes. "There's one tongue that old mossyback understands, Pa—the one Brother Colt talks."

Hugo wore a battered old gun in a homemade holster; he gave it a hard slap.

"Young Wild West," March said dryly. "I told you before to hush that damn talk. You got a man's stature and you wear a man's weapon by choice, as it should be. But by God——"

He checked himself, glancing at Fallon. "The Beckworths seen their share of trouble, John. I served with the Army of Northern Virginia for four years. Had me five brothers; seen every one of 'em die for one side or the other. Hugo and me's the last of our line. I give a vow we'd live for the future. Prosper or hardscrabble, the Beckworths will leave something besides their own shed blood in this world."

"All right," Fallon murmured. "What about Eldridge?"

Old March's hawk eyes narrowed. A sharp word might have been on his tongue, but it didn't get off. His gaze flicked past Fallon to the batwing doors, parting now to admit two men.

Fallon half-turned his head. At once he recognized the man with Kane Eldridge.

Frankie Lomax hadn't changed in eight years, he saw in that brief glance. A small and frail-looking man, he was still as dirty, unshaven, and shabbily dressed as when they'd ridden together for John Chisum in New Mexico's Lincoln County War.

Afterward, the dividing trails of hunted men had split them apart. Though Fallon had heard some time ago that Lomax was now riding for Eldridge, their trails hadn't yet crossed in this valley. It had just been a matter of time, Fallon thought bleakly. You knew that all along, didn't you?

He turned back toward the bar with a pounding heart, bending his head above his glass with only the thinnest hope that he could carry a deception through. His fellow settlers were simple people who had lived staid and respectable lives. Knowing his past, how would they look on it?

And Effie. She hadn't even an inkling of what he had been. That was where the revelation would grind hardest. Effie.

Kane Eldridge halted by Fallon's elbow as Fallon kept his gaze slitted on the mirror behind the bar.

"How-do there, neighbor," Eldridge said mildly, eying Beckworth with an amused and sleepy-eyed malice.

A white-haired, thickset man, Eldridge wore the black broadcloth and bench-made Justins of a prosperous cattleman. He vaunted his love for the land like a banner; it masked and yet mirrored a streak of plain old-fashioned greed.

March Beckworth's faded eyes kindled. "Don't presume to speak to me, sir, after your words of yesterday."

He turned his back on the rancher.

Eldridge showed the edge of a smile, glancing at John Fallon now. "How-do there, son. My man here has been allowing he might know you from som'eres. We come to find out. What do you think of that?"

Unwillingly Fallon turned around, fully facing the two. The blood pounded dismally in his temples.

Frankie Lomax hooked his thumbs in his belt and eyed him unsmilingly. "How you been, Heber?"

"I'm not Heber," Fallon said, his throat dry.

"You're Heber Fallon. You think I don't——" He paused with a slow, mocking nod. "Sorry, Heber. Burying the backtrail, huh? What you want to be called?"

He said it loud enough for every man in the place to take ear.

"My name is John Fallon," Fallon said coldly. "Heber was my brother. He's been dead for five years. Let's leave him that way."

Hugo Beckworth was staring at him with undisguised awe; the other men in the room were watching, starting to talk in low, excited voices.

Who hadn't heard of Heber Fallon, the young daredevil of the Lincoln County Chisum-Murphy feud, who'd ridden with Billy the Kid, then turned against him to join the Kid's enemy, John Chisum? Heber Fallon had ridden unscathed through gauntlets of gunfire in the bloodiest cattle war of the southwest, only to drop mysteriously out of sight at its end, becoming a nebulous figure of legend.

And John Fallon, this quiet-spoken man who neighbored with them, a man quick with a helping hand, yet always one to go unobtrusively about his business, was he only Heber Fallon's *brother?*

Watching the mirror behind the bar, John Fallon could see the question crowd into the men's faces on the heels of their first reaction and now that question was looking at him out of narrowed eyes.

The man, Lomax, had called him Heber, and Lomax

had seemed sure. A man could always be deceived by a strong family resemblance. *Still*——

"Heber Fallon, eh?" mused Kane Eldridge, regarding Fallon with a fresh interest. "Well now, if you're really him, there'd be a place for you on my crew. Triple wages."

"I told you. Heber Fallon is dead."

The rancher made an amused clucking sound with his tongue. "Dead to you maybe, son. Not to the rest of the world." His face hardened slowly. "Better think it over, boy. Man like you ain't used to holding a busted hand. Get in my way, you like to get a heap more busted, hear?"

"Leave the lad be," old March snapped. "Bad enough a man should suffer loose tongues for what some no-account kin of his done. Leave him be."

Eldridge gave him that sleepy look. "You best pull in them horns o' yourn, neighbor, or they will get clipped."

"You don't tell me what to do!" Beckworth rumbled, his gray brows tipping up to his rising wrath. "You think we don't know why you hired this one?" He jerked his shaggy head at Frankie Lomax. "It ain't cow work he's a professional at. And you don't cut wind a whit cleaner, you barn-smelling old bastard!"

"You ever learn to whisper?" said Lomax. "Maybe you ought to be learned to whisper, old man."

"Let it ride, Frankie," Eldridge said, his face empty and unconcerned now. "Benny, give us a drink over here."

Fallon turned and strode from the saloon, a taste of despair in his mouth. He heard Beckworth call after him, "John, wait."

Fallon paused on the long porch of the Stockman's as

Beckworth came out after him, followed by Tom Claussen.

"John, I ain't liking to say this," March Beckworth said. "Mostly I always figured a man should shoot his own dogs. But this here's different."

"Well?" Fallon said harshly.

"We're just folks, us and ours, John. Farming folks. You—I reckon we don't know about you."

Fallon had the sudden feeling that an invisible bar had dropped between him and these men.

"I'll say it just once," he said tightly, "so hear it good. My brother, Heber Fallon, has been in his grave five years. He got shot in the back by a kid looking to make a wrong-way reputation. He lived long enough to get the kid. It was kept quiet because the only man who seen it was a friend of our family. He figured Heber had brought enough shame on the Fallon name; be better to let him drop quietly out of sight. This man buried my brother and told no one but me. Heber and me looked a lot alike, and there was only a year's difference between us. Now that's it."

Beckworth and Claussen exchanged glances; he felt doubt stretch between them.

"Still leaves us in trouble, John," Tom Claussen said slowly. "That man, Lomax, he is a 'warrior' like they hire in the big cattle wars. Man like that takes it in his head he could prod at a man and prod at him till he would have to fight then gun him down and claim self-defense. Supposing Eldridge hired a few more like him——"

"You don't know he'll go that far."

"Well, I'd sure as hell hate to bet my life he won't."

Claussen was riding a tight wire, Fallon thought. All of them were. And it was drawing tighter. "We ain't heard nothing out of Eldridge but talk. He wants to spook you-all and you're letting him. Talk don't fill a man's belly."

"I don't believe that, John," old March growled, "and I don't reckon you do. That man grew up with this country; he took it in his two hands and wrung what he wanted out of it. Might of been a long time ago, but a man like him don't change. Us, we're peaceful folk."

The words felt like a tightening noose; both men were eying him in a calculating way. "So am I, March. So am I."

"Nobody's said otherwise. All the same, a man like this Hebert Fallon could stand to Eldridge on his ground."

"You taken that notion in your head now, have you?" Anger roughened Fallon's voice. "I'm my own brother, am I?"

"We can't say, John," Tom Claussen said dryly. "You answer it."

"I answered it."

"All right, boy," March Beckworth said. "But if it comes to a showdown, there'll be no middle ground. You know that. We'll have to fight. With the only law at a county seat over a hundred miles away, we'll have to fight. And we'll need a man who can lead us."

Fallon shook his head; he rubbed a hand across his eyes as though brushing something away. The smell of dust from the street, the rattle of a harnessed team coming down it—these small things washed against his awareness with an unreasonable clarity.

"Maybe you will," he heard himself say, "but you better know your man before you pick him."

He turned his back on them, quartered across the

street to Jonas' General Store and stalked inside. Effie glanced up from some bolt goods she was examining.

"Mr. Jonas is putting our order together," she said. "Then I'd like you to go over to the feed company with me, John. We need—"

Fallon cut her off curtly. "I'll drive the wagon over and we'll load this stuff. Then we're going home."

Effie did not ask questions, then or later. They were silent on the drive home, and the silence held through supper that evening. There was no hurt withdrawal on Effie's part; she wasn't the kind to sulk. She had wed a seldom-spoken man, a man of moods; she knew it, and knew that nothing would be said till he was ready to say it.

But she knew too that whatever was troubling him ran deeper than anything they had known in their life together. He sensed the bewilderment and concern in her frequent glances at him.

After supper, he walked from the house to the corral and stood in the humid summer twilight, filling his pipe as he let his eye rove across the layout of his homestead. The small, solid barn, the big fenced-off pasture behind it, one field of corn, one of potatoes, and a forty-acre plot of flourishing alfalfa.

It was a good place; it was home: a protest against all that Heber Fallon had stood for made real. Usually he tasted a sense of well-being, of silent thankfulness, just standing this way at the twilight hour and thinking on it.

Tonight only a pressing taste of defeat filled his mouth. For he had his own barren answer, no matter what answer he gave to others. A man couldn't ride so far that a stormy past wouldn't find him out. Seeds of his ruin, of all he had built, lay in the crop of violence that was being sown in this valley. For Eldridge was not bluffing, he was sure. The storm was brewing and was hard on to breaking.

Either way you go, he thought bleakly, you lose. Even if you do nothing, the fat's in the fire. Now Lomax has brought it out, nobody's disposed to believe otherwise, whatever you say.

Still, he could hold stubbornly fast to the white lie on which he had made a new life and put the past he wanted only to forget behind him forever—so far as any action of his was concerned.

Or he could stand up to Eldridge and Lomax and save his neighbors and himself, and spend the rest of his life branded as Heber Fallon, the Lincoln County killer. It wouldn't matter that Governor Lew Wallace had granted amnesty to all the men involved in that Chisum-Murphy feud. It was a brand that wouldn't rub off. His taking up the gun again would surely prove it to others. To Effie.

Effie.

Beside that single consideration, everything else paled. God, if he lost her!

From where he stood, he could see the small kitchen window, a square warm with light, and Effie washing the supper dishes. It was the way he had first seen her, he remembered, when he was riding a grub line west of here and had arrived at her father's place late one evening. There he had seen Effie in warm window light, framed like a picture. A picture that held all he wanted of life or would ever want. . . .

You pegged your own trail all the way, he thought bitterly. You can't blame nobody for that.

And the others? Claussen, Macambridge, Kirkpatrick, Henessey, MacLaine, and old March Beckworth? None were necessarily cowards, but it was a sure-to-hell fact none of 'em were fighters, except maybe old March. He was the only man of them old enough to have seen service in the War of Secession. But March Beckworth, old and war-weary, would not fight for his own.

He'll let me do it for him, though, Fallon thought darkly. What they want ain't a leader, it's an angel. Damn them, I seen my share of it too. Enough of it for ten men. What the hell right do they have to bring it back?

His hand rested on a fence post; he gave it a sudden and savage wrench. The post didn't even tremble. It was braced solid to his strength, and he considered this with a kind of dismal calm. Whatever else, he had sunk his roots here. Roots deep and firm. They would not pull up easily. . . .

Picking up the quick approach of a horse on the town road, Fallon left the corral and tramped up toward the house. The rider's outline was bulky in the thick dusk as he reined up in the yard, and Fallon heard Claussen's shaking voice say, "Whoa. John? That you?"

"Sure."

Claussen swung heavily down and leaned against his saddle leather as if he needed support. "It's . . . oh Jesus."

"What the hell is it?"

"Hugo Beckworth. He got shot by that Lomax."

"Bad?"

"The kid's dead—" Claussen's words came in a rush now. "He was in the Stockman's, drinking up a storm. Lomax began to badger the kid. Called his old man a name and the goddamn fool kid went for that old gun of his. Oh, Christ!"

"Take it easy. You see it happen?"

"No. Old March and I heard the shot as we was across the street talking to my wife. Maybe if one of us had been there, we...." Claussen shook his head and mopped his face with a bandanna. "Jesus. I dunno."

"Old March taking it bad?" Fallon asked softly.

"Worse. Looks like someone kicked the world out from under him. Something else's happened, too. Barney Kirkpatrick is spooked. Says he is got a family to think of. Says he is gonna put his place up for sale."

"That's bad. Time like this, we should all stick fast. Show the vote."

"Yeah, I told him that. But he says his wife is poorly anyways and—hell! you can't talk to a spooked man, John."

"Yeah."

"What the hell we gonna do?"

"You were going home, Tom," Fallon murmured.

Claussen hunched his shoulders, trying to make out his friend's face. "I thought maybe——"

"Go on home, Tom. I'll see you in the morning."

Without another word, Claussen stepped into his saddle and rode out.

Fallon tramped to the barn, went inside, and came out carrying his saddle and something else, something which hadn't seen the light of day in years. It was a smoothly balanced Colt he'd kept carefully cleaned and oiled from force of habit, kept not for use but as a token of man's resolution to change. That resolution, and that alone, he'd wanted to keep strong in his memory.

Now it was holstered snugly against his hip.

He went to the pasture and saddled the sorrel mare, then rode her up by the kitchen porch and dismounted. He moved onto the porch and opened the door.

"Ef," he said gently, "come outside, will you?"

She turned with a sober question in her face. But he said no more, and now she dried her soap-wet hands and stepped out on the porch. Fallon's glance swung to the gleam of a tin can which the dog had wrestled into her little kitchen garden.

"Effie," he said in the same gentle voice, "look here."

He drew the Colt in a blurred motion, sent the can leaping and bounding halfway to the corral in a thunder of gunfire. He turned to face the hushed amazement in his wife's face.

"Now you know me," he murmured. "I lied to you, Ef."

"Lied?"

"The same as. I never told you what I should of told you before we said our vows. You ever hear of Heber Fallon?"

Her eyes moved to the gun and back to his face.

"Did you?" he repeated.

"An outlaw . . . a gunman."

"I'm Heber Fallon. I had a lot of things, bad things, I wanted to leave behind me. I wanted to make myself over into someone else. I came to Wyoming and changed only my first name, figuring it'd be easier to pass myself off as Heber's brother in case anyone ever knew my face. Nobody ever did . . . till today. Eldridge's guntipper, Frankie Lomax? We knew each other in New Mexico."

"But," she whispered, "why tell me this now?"

"Because Lomax killed Hugo Beckworth today in the Stockman's."

"Oh—"

"Because our neighbors are starting to spook. Because they ain't fighting men and because men with families to worry about have got no edge at all." Fallon scrubbed a hand slowly over his face. "And mostly because I can settle this whole business. Can settle it for good and all. Tonight."

Effie swayed against the door frame, stunned by this upending, in a few, fleeting seconds, of her whole small world. She began to lift her hands, then dropped them to her sides.

"John," she said helplessly. "John. . . ."

"Heber. It's Heber, Effie. You'll think about that hereafter."

Fallon reached down to catch up the sorrel mare's trailing reins, then straightened and looked at her. The planes of his face briefly softened. "I lied to you once. But our life here was never a lie, Ef. Not with all you gave me and I tried to give you. You think of that, Effie. Hold fast to it no matter what happens."

He did not touch her, but swung away quickly and mounted the sorrel. Then, with a quick turn, he left the yard and headed down the darkening road to Crane's Crossing.

It had to be done that way, he thought. The telling abrupt and clean, like the stroke of a knife. And with it, maybe, he had cut off all that gave a man's life meaning. But if he had, he couldn't go up against what he must tonight, and knowing it, want to live.

Fallon was sure of that much. And he wanted to live. He had never wanted it more. If a hurtfulness was to come out, let it come out when time had cushioned the first shock for both of them.

He rode to Crane's Crossing without a pause, except to reload and check his gun. Leaving his mare at the tie rail by the courthouse, he crossed to the Stockman's.

On a Saturday night, most of Eldridge's crew, including Lomax, would be in town. He would have stayed after killing young Beckworth. That was Frankie's way, the quiet brag that said more than any words.

Fallon tried to recall what he knew of the man's drinking habits and remembered that Lomax could nurse a shot glassful of whiskey along all evening; he had never been a drinker. You couldn't depend on liquor slowing him.

A number of horses were tied at the Stockman's long rail; a boozy blare of sound spilled out past the batwing doors. Fallon tramped across the porch and parted the doors and halted.

There was a scattering of cowhands at the bar. One of them was trying to play a tune on the battered piano at the back, but the notes died under his fingers as he glanced toward Fallon.

Heber Fallon. Word had gotten around.

Fallon crossed to the bar. "Whiskey," he said.

Benny carefully wiped his hands on his soiled apron, eying Fallon and then his gun. The influx of settlers had added to the Stockman owner's business, but he'd never made any bones about being a cowman partisan.

"Don't recall as I seen you pack a hogleg before."

"Well, like the Book says, Benny, there is no new thing under the sun."

Benny eyed him balefully, then gave a slight tip of his head toward the Wineglass men. "You sure you want to drink here tonight?"

"That's right." Fallon's tone held the politest of edged suggestions that the owner mind his own business.

Glowering wordlessly, Benny set a bottle and glass on the bar before him. Every man in the place watched Fallon stonily as he carried the bottle and glass to a rear table beneath the balcony running the width of the back wall.

A Wineglass cowboy named Hance was already sitting there. Seventeen and beardless, he was sipping a whiskey with awkward self-consciousness.

Fallon stopped in front of him and said flatly, "Move."

"What?"

Fallon set the bottle and glass gently on the tabletop and rested his knuckles on it, leaning forward. "Light a shuck. Drag it. Hit the trail. That clear enough for you?"

He didn't figure, unsure of himself as Hance seemed, that he'd need to press the point. He had no taste for shaming the boy, but he wanted this vantage of the room. Hance got up and walked to the bar, muttering.

Fallon hauled the single chair around so he could face the whole room, sat, poured a drink, and left it untouched before him. Two Wineglass men quickly downed their drinks and walked out—to find Lomax, he knew.

Yes sir, word had surely got around.

Lomax would be unable to refuse a plain challe[nge] And he would be curious as to how Heber Fallon's fa[mous] prowess with a gun stood up after years of disuse[. The] old riddle of a gunman's pride: it had been so wit[h Fal-]lon once.

This is how it will come, Fallon thought, and [sat] back to watch the batwing doors and wait. The

17

in line; men began clearing off from it, leaving the Stockman's one by one, trying not to seem in too much of a hurry. Benny vanished through a back door.

The batwings were still rocking to the last man's exit when Lomax came pushing through them. He moved halfway across the room and halted. He was smoking one of the Mexican cigars he'd always favored.

"Want a drink, Heber?"

Fallon stood slowly, and stepped around the table and away from it. "Why," he said gently, "I figured I would offer you one, Frankie." He lifted his hand toward the bottle and glass.

Lomax smiled. "A friendly drink, huh? That it, Heber?"

"That's it."

"We sit down, we pour a drink, we talk over old times. Sounds right pleasant. After that, Heber—"

He let the question hang.

"After that, there's other places. Other towns. You'll find one to your taste."

Lomax's smile widened. "Got no belly for it any more, have you?"

Fallon shook his head slowly. "I don't want this, Frankie. But don't make a mistake."

Lomax flipped the cigar to the floor between them.

"You been a farmer too long, Heber," he said, and went for his gun.

Fallon's first shot flung Lomax around against the bar. he little gunman clung to the bar-top and came around t, bringing up his unfired gun. Fallon's second shot ve him backward to hit the floor in an arm-flung vl. He didn't move again.

on took a couple of slow steps forward, watching

the doors again, ready for anything. As a man came suddenly through them, he brought up the gun, then lowered it.

"March——"

Old Beckworth was hatless, his white hair a cloudy nimbus about his head, a long-barreled shotgun in his hands. In that moment, his eyes burning like coals, he looked like a patriarchal figure stepped from the Old Testament, wrathy and towering.

"Don't take another step, John!"

Fallon had one wild moment of disbelief, seeing him bring up the shotgun. But it swung to point high above Fallon's head, and now March pulled one trigger.

A man's scream echoed the deafening roar of the old Greener.

Fallon moved swiftly from under the balcony, wheeling then, his glance stabbing upward. Kane Eldridge was sinking down behind the balcony railing, holding his blood-soaked shoulder and arm, sobbing with pain as a six-gun slipped from his fingers. One more step, Fallon realized, and he would have made a straight-down target for Eldridge.

The doors parted and a half-dozen Wineglass men were herded inside. Behind them came Tom Claussen with a Winchester in hand, his round face jut-jawed and determined. Don MacLaine and Archie Macambridge were right behind him.

Claussen came across the room to Fallon and touched his arm gingerly. "You all right, John?"

"Sure. I'm all right. This your idea, Tom?"

"Well, I done some tall thinking tonight before I reached home. Then I got my rifle and rode back to your place. Effie told me you'd gone to town, so I come on fast. Met up with March and Don and Archie coming from March's place. Seems they all had the same idea."

Looking at his friend's round, perspiring, jut-jawed face, Fallon thought, that is all of it. A hundred Eldridges can throw all hell at us and not budge us out now, any of us.

"John. . . ." Claussen took off his hat and drew his sleeve across his face, peering squint-eyed at Fallon. "I reckon you can say it now. The truth."

"I'm Heber Fallon."

I'm Heber Fallon. Said all at once, it was that easy to say.

As he stepped out of the Stockman's, a wagon came rolling down the street from the town's north end. Fallon pulled up, recognizing Effie's blue print dress before anything else. And then she was off the wagon's high seat and running, running to him, and she was close and dear in his arms.

He talked to her quietly for a time, and her trembling ceased. She stirred softly in his arms, her voice muffled against his shoulder. "All that is done, John. We can forget about it."

He tipped up her face. It was tear-streaked, but her eyes were firm. "Ef, it's Heber now. You're Mrs. Heber Fallon."

"Heber," she whispered. "I can say it. It's only a name, isn't it? Heber. . . ."

THE CACHE AND THE CONVICT

Her eyes dry and hard, Mattie Ingersol looked up at the big stranger on the pinto. "My pa's ailing, mister . . . ailing something fierce. Would you come have a look at him?"

Hardly moving his great frame, the man turned his head to peer across the parched flats over which he'd come. Then he looked back at her. His broad, pale face had something of the Indian in its still watchfulness. Yet Mattie sensed he was a man not altogether easy in his mind. He wore rough jeans, a cotton shirt, and a battered horse thief hat which he took off now so he could pull a grimy sleeve across his sweaty face. A bone-handled .44 was thrust in the waistband of his pants.

"I am heading directly south, miss. Have a long way to go yet. Just stopped to fill my canteen and maybe collect my bearings."

"He is pretty bad off, mister. I don't reckon it would put you out so much to come have a look."

The big man clapped his hat back on. "I got no way for ministering to the sick." He stared at her face a moment longer, then swung down off the pinto. "All right. I'll have a look at him."

Mattie's shoulders stirred with the relief of a small victory; she raised a brown hand to push the heavy dark hair back from her face. "In the shack," she said.

The big man stepped to the narrow doorway of the sag-roofed adobe, filling it, and paused to adjust his glare-weary eyes to the interior gloom. He crossed the cramped little room to the cot where Rafe Ingersol's frail form lay. Mattie leaned a hand against the door frame, letting it take her weight, resting her face sideways against her arm. She felt a little dizzy, tired to the bone; she hadn't slept for most of three days.

"I reckon he is just wore out," she heard herself say. "Wandered the desert most of thirty years hunting gold. It was a bigger fever'n the one he is running now. It just wore him out."

"Miss," the big man said.

"We never had no home, you know. It's allus been drift here, drift there. Ma left us after it wore thin on her. That there was a long time ago."

"Miss."

"What is it?"

"Ain't nothing nobody can do here. Your pa's dead."

The man moved back from the cot and Mattie came to stand by it, looking down at her father's waxy face and staring eyes. She didn't know how long she stood that way. When she turned at last, the big man was still there, just watching.

"Maybe I can trouble you again," she said huskily. "He is got to be buried. It should be right away, all this heat, and don't reckon I can manage it. I am wore out myself, mister."

Again there was that long break of hesitation. Then he let his shoulders settle in a kind of resigned way. "If he prospected, I reckon there is a shovel about. All right."

After Mattie had wrapped her father in his cot blankets, the man carried him outside and set the body down where she told him, in the shade of a big rock. Then he began to break the stony ground, driving the shovel in with long, powerful strokes. After five minutes of it, he paused and stripped off his wet shirt, glancing her way.

"You take it mighty quiet."

Mattie lowered her eyes. "I knew a long time he was dying. It's gone hard these weeks, thinking on it. What I got to think about now is living."

The man gave a curt nod as if that made sense, and resumed his digging. She left him then, walking a short distance away from the place. When she was hidden by a cloudy green forest of mesquite, she dropped to her knees and let the tears come, the harsh sobs wracking her body.

She was composed and dry-eyed when she walked back to the 'dobe. By then the man had the grave dug; together they lowered her father into it. Mattie watched him fill the grave, working steadily in the thick afternoon heat, his movements ponderous and strong, without wasted motion.

His torso was great-shouldered and bull-chested; muscle squirmed and flexed across his back. A lick of sandy hair fell over his forehead and clung damply there. She wondered at his paleness in this land of weather-darkened men, even his face and hands were many shades lighter than her own.

When the grave was nearly filled, she recognized the drag of heat exhaustion in his movements. "You are just about done up," she said primly, and walked over to grasp the shovel handle. "I'll finish this."

The man let go of the shovel and straightened, tugging a bandanna from his hip pocket and mopping his brow. Then he eyed her at some length, squinting his reddened eyes. For all the strong control that a hard life had beat into her, Mattie felt her face go warm.

She wasn't pretty, she knew; the over-resolute jaw and blunt features of her father lay on her face. Yet she had a kind of clear-skinned and healthy glow about her that people noticed. A tall, strongly made girl, she was wideshouldered and full-bosomed; she was too robust ever to be called slender, but compact and lean, and she moved well.

The stranger shrugged, showing he was a practical man, and sat down nearby to roll a cigarette. Tired as she was, Mattie worked with a strong, unslackening rhythm that helped channel off the bitterness of her thoughts. Finally she smoothed the grave over and straightened up, feeling her blouse cling sweatily to her supple shoulders and the jutting hills of her breasts. A vagrant touch of hot wind pressed the faded skirt against her round, sturdy thighs.

Glancing at the man as he sat smoking a thin cigarette and giving her an unabashed scrutiny through the smoke, Mattie felt the heat rise to her face again. She set her firm jaw. I am a lone woman and he is getting ideas. Well, if he thinks this service gives him some rights, he will be a sorry shorthorn.

She met his eyes boldly. "My name is Matilda Ingersol. What's yours?"

"Carrighar," he said in an absent voice. "Les Carrighar."

A quick scowl crossed his face; abruptly he stood up and pulled on his shirt. It's like he didn't mean to say that, Mattie thought wonderingly—say his name. . . .

He took a final drag on his cigarette, ground it under his boot, and glanced at the molten splash of sunset above the gaunt hills to the west. Then he muttered, "Hell," softly and disgustedly, and gave her a withdrawn look.

"Won't get much farther before it comes dark. Mind if I lay over here tonight? Can make camp under them cottonwoods yonder."

A protest welled almost to Mattie's lips, but she let it die unsaid. Whether he had ideas or no, this courtesy was surely his due. There was good water here and good grass for his animal; he'd have a hard time finding as good for the next fifty miles south.

"You are welcome to stay," she said stonily.

She went into the shack and fixed supper, watching Carrighar through the open door as he watered his horse, threw off the saddle and bridle, and turned the animal loose in the deep grass in the cottonwood shade. Afterward he washed up at the spring. All this he did methodically, then sat down under the trees to smoke.

Presently, when supper was ready, Mattie felt obligated to invite him in to eat.

Carrighar wolfed down a good meal of beans and biscuits, finished it off with two cups of strong black coffee, and settled back in his chair with a cigarette. Mattie ate slowly, feeling his steady gaze on her, intent but not brash, just bemused and thoughtful.

"You're in kind of a fix, ain't you?"

"I reckon I am." She continued to eat, not looking up from her plate.

"Well, you can't just stay on in the middle o' nowhere, your pa gone. Ain't you got no kin?"

"Could be my ma's alive somewhere."

"Got no horse to take you out o' here, I seen that."

"I used to have one. A lion got him one night. There's only Pa's burro he used to fetch supplies from Silver City."

"That's dandy," he grunted. "Don't matter which way you strike out from here, you are a wide spit shy of the nearest settlement." He slanted a dour look at her. "And you can't go with me. My animal can't take double in country like this. And I ain't exactly in a way to be saddled with no female."

Her eyes came up, bright and hard. "I don't recall you got asked, mister."

"You didn't get offered, neither." He flicked ash into his cup. "Don't seem likely you'd have any neighbors way out here."

"No. Jack Riordan mostly. He is a gold hunter drifts by now and again."

"What's now and again?"

"Maybe once a week. He's about due around."

"He be minded to help you out? See you to a settlement?"

She thought of Jack Riordan and his braggy, strutty ways with no enthusiasm. "I reckon he might do that."

"Well, you got no problem then."

"No," Mattie said, trying to fight the sarcasm out of her voice. "Not a one."

Twilight was thickening, the golden light turning plum-colored. Mattie got up to light the battered lamp that swung on a wire from a beam. As its sickly glow spread through the room, Carrighar said idly, "What about money? How are you fixed?"

She gave him a guarded look. "Well enough, I reckon."

"Could be your pa had a cache laid by some'eres. Desert rats like him, they like as not keep some o' their dust laid aside."

Mattie didn't reply.

Carrighar shrugged. "Well, if you know where——"

He broke off to the sound of a horse approaching the shack, the hoofbeats soft in the quiet. As she got up and moved to the doorway, Mattie saw Carrighar's hand stir close to that bone-stocked .44 in his belt.

It was Jack Riordan. He dismounted and threw his reins over his horse's head and swaggered toward her, a tall slope-shouldered man with a bantam-cock strut. A gold tooth glimmered in the ambush of his dirty yellow beard. Though she had little use for the man, Mattie felt a wash of relief at his arrival.

"How-do, Mattie. Was close by, so thought I would camp over by your spring. How is ole Rafe doing? I see a strange horse picketed yonder. You got company?"

She stepped aside to let Riordan enter. He and Carrighar sized each other up in the careful way men did at first meeting in this lonely country. A thread of tension stretched between them on the instant. Mattie felt it with a sense of disquiet as she said their names.

"Pleased t' make your acquaintance, sir," Riordan said toothily, stepping to the table and extending his hand. "Carrighar, hey? Thought it might be Smith, something like that. Y'know, John Smith? Heh heh heh."

"It might at that," Carrighar said agreeably.

He stayed relaxed in his chair, but his eyes were as alert as a cat's. Mattie felt the danger in him then: that if he saw the need for it, he would move as sudden and quick as a cat.

"Heh heh heh," Riordan laughed. "How 'bout a cup of that coffee for ole Jack, Mattie?" His glance flicked to her father's empty cot. "Ole Rafe, he up and around again, hey? Where'bouts is he?"

Mattie told him.

"Aw, sho now. Ole Rafe. That is purely a shame."

Soberly clucking his tongue and shaking his head, Riordan sat at the table and took the cup of coffee she handed him. "Thankee, girl." He swilled the hot brew down, smacking his lips. "Just traveling through, I take it, Mr. Carrighar? For points south, I reckon?"

"Points south," Carrighar agreed.

His tone held a polite and steely hint that the matter wasn't to be enlarged on, and Mattie felt a thin anger at Jack Riordan. She knew little about men, but she knew Riordan's way of slyly baiting another. A man like this stranger wouldn't bait easily.

"Yeah," Riordan drawled, sliding his half-lidded glance to the girl. "Wouldn't be a mite o' firewater about the place, would there? Your daddy kept a jug he lugged out once or twice when I come visiting. Heh, looks like it on the shelf yonder."

Reluctantly Mattie got the jug and filled his cup as he held it out. She gave Carrighar a questioning look; he shook his head. Riordan took a long swig.

"Whee-oo, if that ain't pure lightning for a man's craw. Well, girl, anyways you won't have no worldly worries for a spell, not with that pile your daddy put aside over the years."

Mattie gave Carrighar a swift, apprehensive look. His large frame was still slack in the chair, his eyes fixed sleepily on the smoke of his cigarette.

"That don't come to so much, I reckon. We allus lived make-do, Jack, you know that."

"Heh heh heh——" Riordan drained his cup. "Listen,

girl, ole Rafe knew the places. Never scrabbled him up no big strike, but he done all right, 'y God, over the long pull. 'Course he was plenty closemouthed on't. Only bragged about it once, when he was likkered up. Seems he been salting it away for years, holding out what he needed for grub stakes and the like—"

Mattie's mouth was dry; her palms felt cold. "Jack—" she said, fighting to hold her voice steady, "would you kindly step outside with me a minute?"

"Oh, sure. Sure, honey girl. I be tickled to. Heh heh heh."

Dusk had settled over the desert, filling the pockets and swales and pooling in thick shadows beneath the stand of cottonwoods well away from the cabin. Mattie led Riordan under the trees, then wheeled on him, shaking with anger.

"Jack, what you up to, anyway? You trying—"

"Keep your voice down, girl."

"You hush up and hear me! I don't hanker to get robbed and murdered on account of your big mouth! I don't know nothing about that stranger."

"Whoa, girl, easy there. Heh heh, listen now, *I* know something, all right."

"What's that mean?"

"Well, Mattie girl, I just come from Silver City. This Les Carrighar, he busted out o' Yuma Prison two weeks ago. Ever' lawman in the terr'tory is got word on him. I reckon he been working his way south slow and easy, laying low a lot o' the time. He is headed for Mexico, you bet."

Mattie was aghast. "You *knew* that and you went running off to his face about Pa's gold?"

"Listen, honey girl——" Riordan hunched a little forward, a wave of whiskey-smell hitting her face. "Just don't you worry no-ways. Ole Jack is got that yahoo's number, you bet. I ain't a-skeered none o' him and he knows it now. He ain't gonna molest you whilst I am about, and I mean to camp right smack here till he is gone his way. Which I make will be goddamn quick now."

She stared at him. "Why? 'Cause you think he is a-scared of you? *You?*"

Her tone singed his touchy pride like a cholla sting. His hand shot out and grasped her wrist. "Don't you do that, girl. Don't you never laugh at Jack Riordan."

She twisted with all her strength against his hold, but couldn't break it. "Jack," she said in a wintry voice, "you don't unhand me in short order, I am going to bust you one in the mouth."

Riordan gave a shout of laughter. " 'Y God, you would at that, give you a chance. Trouble with you, Mattie, is you never had no man in your time. Now have you?"

"No——" She gave a vicious yank against his grip, "—but then I never seen none about."

"I'll show you, 'y God!"

Suddenly his arms went around her, pinning her arms. She fought him wildly, desperate to escape the press of his scratchy beard and whiskey-stink, but he was bear-strong.

"Let go! Let go a me, you—"

"Do it," Carrighar said gently.

His dark form bulked close beside them. With a startled curse, Riordan flung Mattie aside and came pivoting around. Carrighar's arm lashed up like a striking snake; it hit with the solid crunch of an ax blade. Riordan was bowled over backward.

Mattie had lit on her shoulder with a bruising impact. She rolled to a sitting position, seeing Riordan crawl wobby-legged to his feet. Then she saw him lunge, a wink of steel in his hand, and she let out a screech.

Riordan swung the knife.

Carrighar let out a hard, angry grunt, and chopped a fist low into Riordan's belly. A groan of pure agony left Jack Riordan as he went down in the grass, bowed double with pain, his face pinched with it. Carrighar picked up the knife. He prodded Riordan with a foot.

"You wore out your welcome, big mouth. Soon's you're able to, get."

He turned and headed back for the adobe, pausing by Riordan's mount to yank his carbine from its saddle boot. Carrying it, he went into the shack.

Mattie scrambled to her feet, shaking with a confused rush of feelings. Mr. Carrighar would never draw a blue ribbon for gallantry. All the same, he had saved her bacon for sure. Slowly, her knees trembling, she walked back to the adobe.

Carrighar had turned up the lamp flame and now he sat at the puncheon table, using Riordan's knife to cut away his blood-soaked right sleeve.

"Oh," Mattie said, and added weakly, "he cut you."

"Looks that way. Maybe you would be good enough to boil some water and get me something for a bandage." He peered at his arm. "That is going to require some sewing."

Mattie stoked up the fire in the mud oven. As she set a pot of water to boil, Riordan came stumbling to the doorway, holding his belly. His face was bloodless and sickly.

"You son of a bitch," he whispered. "You taken my saddle gun."

"Another word out o' you," Carrighar said softly, "and you'll get it fed down your gullet butt first. You're damn lucky you are just out hardware, mister. Now you fork that nag out o' here."

Riordan stood staring a moment, then turned and stumbled to his horse. He made it into the saddle on his third try. The sounds of his going faded in the night.

Mattie washed Carrighar's arm, treated it with bluestone and sweet oil, and sewed up the six-inch gash.

"You done real nice," he said, reaching for his tobacco and papers. "Thanks."

"Reckon I'm the one who's beholden."

Mattie felt shy and flushed; she avoided his eyes as she began clearing the table, carrying dishes to the makeshift wooden counter. He rolled a cigarette dexterously with one hand, and then he said idly, "What-all you tell him? Must of been something fierce, the way he riled."

"It wasn't nothing."

"It wasn't, huh?" He snapped a match alight on his thumbnail. "Just a pretty passel o' nothing."

Mattie put her back to him, clattering dishes into the pan. "You got no call to talk so smart. He is proud and he is mean. I was you, I wouldn't stay around here. He will be back."

"Don't reckon he'll hurry about it, seeing his teeth are pulled."

She glanced over her shoulder, seeing a faint grin crook his mouth through a swirl of smoke; he nodded at Riordan's knife and rifle on the table.

"But——" She bit her lip.

"Yeah?"

"Well, he said something. Maybe it was a lie. He could of been—"

Carrighar said quietly, dryly, "I'm a jailbird flew the coop. He tell you that?"

She gave a small, jerky nod.

"Well, that's gospel enough. But I never got put there for doing a woman harm. That ain't my style."

"What was it then?"

He eyed her in that strange, musing way, as though he hadn't heard the question. Mattie felt gooseflesh ripple her skin, as if small, cold fingers had brushed it. Yet suddenly she was not afraid of him. She felt kind of flustered and excited, but not fearful.

"I mean, supposing he goes to the law and fetches 'em back here? I was you, I wouldn't be sitting around."

"Nearest law is two days from here. I'll be gone in the morning."

Mattie's face burned under his steady gaze. She swung her back to him, plunging her hands into the dishwater. "I don't care what you do."

"Glad to hear that—"

He spoke lazily and very softly, and she heard him stand up now. He was coming up behind her and she felt weak and nerveless, unable to move. Her heart was pounding wildly and she couldn't stir a muscle. She felt his hands on her arms, bare where she'd rolled up her sleeves to tend him, and he gently turned her to face him. He was smiling a little, his eyes full of little kindling lights, and then he kissed her. His face was unshaven and rough, but he wasn't; he wasn't rough at all.

Of a sudden, though, she was afraid again.

Mattie made a little squirm of noise in her throat, trying to push him away. She beat with her fists at his shoulders and arms, but the blows slid harmlessly off. Backed as she was against the counter by his bulk, she was practically helpless.

He didn't let go of her till he was ready. Then there was a different look in his face, brooding, almost frowning. Not angry, but wondering.

She scrubbed a hand across her mouth. "You're as bad as Jack——"

"No," he said. "No, ma'am. You don't know anything about a man, do you?"

"And you, you, I suppose, know all there is to about women!"

"I reckon I just thought I did."

His smile was rueful; his eyes held a curious and baffled look. He turned and walked to the door, then came to a stop and eyed it. "No bar," he said. "No lock." He turned back toward her. She retreated a step sideways, thrusting out an arm as if to ward him off.

He halted, saying dryly, "Reckon I'll sleep outside tonight." He pulled the .44 from his belt and held it out to her. Mechanically, she took it. "I 'low you wouldn't sleep much," he said in a dry and enigmatic voice. "Might be that'll help."

He walked out of the shack, pulling the door softly to behind him.

Mattie turned the lamp up and crawled into her cot fully dressed, holding the gun against her skirt and watching the door, listening for any odd sound. After a time her high-strung nerves and muscles relaxed. Her chaotic thoughts came together and focused on a man's strong arms, his lips, his rough beard, and a fierce pounding began in her veins.

Oh Lordy, don't be a fool. He is a convict man and for all you know he killed somebody. And he is leaving here; he'll be gone and that's that.

She pressed a hand over her eyes and felt a warm wetness puddle against it. Mattie Ingersol was toughbred; she had never been a crying sort. But she had cried once today, and now she cried again, painfully suppressing her sobs to silent, jerking spasms and a lot of tears.

She came awake suddenly in the breaking dawn. For a moment her mind was a blank. Then she remembered, and rising quickly, went to the door, her heart pounding as she opened it just a crack.

Carrighar was leaning against a tree, his back to her, studying the sun-shimmering desert to the south. Mattie felt a quickening gladness, and then she shut the door and wheeled around, rubbing the gooseflesh that had come up on her arms at the sight of him. Oh, Lordy! What a fool she was. He'd be gone directly enough, and it was for nothing but the best. . . .

She set about fixing breakfast, her nerve-ends alert for any sound that might indicate he was preparing to depart. Presently the door opened behind her.

"Morning. Chance of a bite to eat?"

"Suit yourself," she said coldly. "I thought you was in a rush to be going."

"I'll be on my way soon enough. Listen here, what'll you do about getting away from this place? You won't be going with Riordan, I expect."

"Don't you fret your head about it, Mr. Jailbird. It ain't no worry of yours."

"It ain't, rightly," he agreed.

She set the meal out and they ate in silence. Finished, Carrighar said, "I could use another cup o' coffee."

She brought the pot and poured, and felt his strong measuring gaze on her face. "I'm thinking," he said abruptly, "as you got no place to go, that we might strike a bargain."

"Bargain?"

"I am headed Mexico way. A body can make do below the border on next to nothing, but I am flat busted. Now if your pa had a goodly cache of gold about, it might stretch a long way for a long time—for both of us."

Mattie stared at him, the coffeepot poised in her hand, the blood rising hot in her face. Then she slammed the pot down on the table. "Is that your 'bargain'? My pa's gold for the company of a jailbird and—and Lord God knows what else? No thank you!"

Carrighar scowled. "You don't know beans about the way of things. How old are you?"

"What's that got to? . . . Going on nineteen, if it's any business of yours."

"Well, I was a year shy of nineteen when I got mixed up with a hardcase crew that set out to rob a bank. We got shot to pieces trying and I got caught. The judge, he said my youth was no good excuse. I was a smart-mouth brat too big for my britches and I made the mistake o' sassing him."

Carrighar's mouth pulled tight and bitter. "All the same, I never figured that should of bought me a ten-year sentence to Yuma. I served six years of it before they give me outside work. I'd behaved myself and maybe I could of got some time knocked off. But I couldn't stand it no longer. I made my break and I made it clean." His eyes were slate-hard. "I ain't going back, ain't spending one more day o' my life in that hellhole. They ever catch up, they won't take me alive. You understand?"

Mattie nodded, slowly and numbly.

"Well," Carrighar raised a shoulder and let it fall, "that is the straight of my story. I 'low it makes a damn thin offering for a good girl. There's girls a man could offer less to and not blush for it. But not you, Mattie." He looked down at his big hands, closing and unclosing them. "I was a wild kid, not a bad one. If I turned bad, it was that place I left that done it. A man can make himself over. A new start, a new life. We can have it together, if you're willing."

Mattie averted her eyes. "You are wanted by the law. You admit it could catch up."

"It could happen, even in Mexico. The Arizona Rangers and the *rurales* have got a working agreement between 'em. Man can change his name, his whole way of life, but there's no guarantees. Thing is, a man with money can find ways to throw the smartest law-dog off the scent. I kept my ears open in Yuma, learned a heap about things like that. A man can always make his way the better, he's got money enough."

Mattie shook her head dismally. "I don't reckon," she said almost inaudibly. "Thank you all the same."

"Sure." A studied blankness dropped over his voice. "You got no reason to believe me, that's sure. Or trust me."

"It ain't that. What you are proposing is wrong. Plain wrong, that's all."

"Wrong how?" His brows drew together. "It's a two-way bargain. Maybe I didn't make it clear. I am offering you a husband, if you want him. A man who'll work for you and care for you. I'm a loyal man too, Mattie Ingersol. I never welshed or cheated on a body in my life. Reckon I would still get the best of the deal, but for whatever it means, I am putting all my cards on the table. A man can't do more."

She gave him a straight-eyed look now. "There is no talk of feeling in all this. That's what's wrong."

He scowled. "Feeling?"

"You for me, me for you. We ain't cattle, we are folks —people. We don't just sell ourselves to each other. I reckon you don't know how a woman, a good woman, feels about something like that."

"My mother was one, Mattie. I reckon I do." His voice softened. "That could come—the feeling. But you got to give it time. Plenty folks have started with no more, good folks who were in a fix and had no choice but make the best of things. That's where you and me are."

Mattie was a realist, and now she gave a slow, bitter nod. "Yes, I can see that. Just living is taking chances, ain't it? But there's one chance I can't take, Les Carrighar."

"What's that?"

"I can't take the chance I will get a feeling for you and then, one day, a lawman will come to take you away. I couldn't live with you knowing that, wondering when it will come. I couldn't and I won't!"

Her voice had a half-shrill note in her ears; she swung away to hide the wet blurring of her eyes. "You better go. Just get your horse and ride out of here. Go on!"

There was a moment's silence. Then his chair scraped

back and she heard him tramp out. Mattie braced herself, drawing up her shoulders. She was going to walk to that door and watch him depart. Above all, she was going to shed not one tear.

Anyway, not till he was out of sight.

As she started to turn, she saw his .44 gun lying on the cot. She picked it up and went outside. Carrighar was throwing his saddle on his mount and she started toward him, saying, "Don't forget—"

A rifle shot crashed out.

Carrighar's horse thief hat spun away from his head. The convict reacted at once, slashing a hand across his horse's rump and sending the startled animal away toward the brush.

He yelled at Mattie, "Get inside!"

But she stood rooted to the spot as Carrighar, yards away from the shack, launched himself in a driving run for the nearby rock that marked her father's grave. A second bullet kicked up a geyser of dust close to his heels. Six feet from the rock, the third bullet drove Carrighar's right leg from under him.

He skidded on his face and belly and then his head met the rock. He lay sprawled against it, unmoving.

Jack Riordan came tramping out of the forest of mesquite many yards away, rifle nestled in the crook of his arm. He was cackling like a loony.

"Wait right there, Mattie girl. Ole Jack is come back for you, heh heh heh—"

Mattie wasn't twelve feet from the shack. She wheeled and ran back inside, slamming the door. For a moment she leaned against it, weak with fury and fear.

Riordan had had another rifle cached somewhere. And

Carrighar—was he dead? Riordan would try to make sure. The thought galvanized her to action. She mustn't let Riordan get close to the fallen man. . . .

Quickly she opened the door a crack.

Riordan was nowhere in sight.

Then she heard his amused cackle from the mesquite; he'd retreated back to its cover. "Aw right, Mattie girl, your friend ain't in no way to do you a lick of good. So let's dicker sensible, you 'n' me. You open the door 'n' throw out that Winchester o' mine and your pa's ole Henry, too. Then we'll dicker. Hey?"

Mattie pulled the door shut, her mind racing. Riordan hadn't seen Carrighar's pistol. She'd been holding it at her side; a fold of her skirt had hidden it. But she must playact the situation for all it was worth, let him believe he had her in a bind.

She waited, not replying.

Riordan bawled impatiently, "Come on, girl! Don't stall me. I am holding every chip in this game. Your friend there, he's bad hurt, mebbe dying. You want him to live, you gonna come to taw with ole Jack. It's my game now, Mattie, all the way!"

She opened the door slightly. "All right, Jack," she called hoarsely. "All right. I am throwing the guns out."

Riordan's rifle went out the door first, then Pa's. Mattie held back, leaving the door a couple of inches ajar, watching around its edge. She cocked the .44.

She saw Riordan emerge from the mesquite, mounted now, gigging his horse toward the shack. His hat brim made a black shadow across his face; the rifle was balanced on the pommel of his saddle. He hauled up his horse a short distance away.

"You come outa there now, girl. Come out where I can see you."

Mattie stood back a yard from the door, knowing the shack's dark interior would hide her movements as, holding the .44 two-handed now, she cocked it and lined Riordan's head and shoulders along its sights through the crack in the door.

She pulled the trigger.

The heavy weapon bucked in her grasp; its roar was deafening in the room. A cloud of powder smoke cut off her view, but she could hear Riordan cursing wildly. Quickly she thrust open the door to take a full view of the yard.

Riordan was still in the saddle, fighting to get his plunging horse under control. Blood streaked the animal's head; it was only grazed, but the wound was enough to send it into a panic.

Mattie brought the .44 up, trying to take aim against the horse's crazed gyrations.

Riordan snapped a glance at her, swore again, and fired his rifle wildly, one-handed. The bullet slammed into the door frame; a shard of wood flew into Mattie's face. The pain made her shrink back, pawing at her cheek. In the same instant, Riordan achieved partial control over his horse; the animal thundered away, tearing into the mesquite.

Mattie crouched in the doorway as the sound of Riordan's horse crashing through the brush died away. For long seconds she was numb with pain and shock, straining her ears against the hot and windless silence. Then she pulled herself together, swiping a hand across her bleeding cheek. Fortunately the wound was just a cut.

She had to get Carrighar inside the shack before Riordan came back. She'd missed her golden chance, used up her sole advantage, and now she must work quickly. She ran out to the convict's sprawled form and, tugging fiercely, turned him over on his back.

He groaned softly.

He lived, thank the Lord. Get him inside, bring him around somehow before Riordan returns, Mattie thought fiercely. Carrighar would know what to do; this she felt with blind and utter confidence.

Mattie rammed the pistol awkwardly into the waistband of her skirt, then bent and grabbed the unconscious man under the arms and threw her weight against her heels, pulling. Lord, he was an ox of a man. Desperately she jerked and tugged, moving him along by inches toward the shack door. Sweat broke on her face and hit her eyes in a stinging wash.

"That's far enough, honey girl."

She let go of Carrighar and spun wildly, swiping at her eyes. Riordan trotted into view out of the mesquite, smiling like a bland pixie. "Now you drop that hogleg, hear? You lift 'er with your left hand and let 'er fall."

Mattie did as she was told.

Riordan advanced, rifle loosely pointed, cackling to himself. "What I done, I jist dropped off that nag and let 'im run, then hustled back here. How dumb you think ole Jack is, kid?" He pulled up a few feet away, glancing down at the hurt man. "Ain't that a sack o' pure hell, now."

"Jack——" She forced the words from a cottony throat. "Leave him alive. Leave him alive and I'll do whatever you want."

"Sure you will, sweetie pie. Looks like the critter's half dead anyways. Let's talk out that dicker I mentioned, now."

"I got to help him first."

"Uh-uh. You leave the bastard be. I let you save his scalp; he's like to be hell-fire to lift mine." He waggled the rifle, running his gaze over her, head to toe. "I got diff'rent plans—for you 'n' me 'n' that dust o' your pappys. Whereabouts he cache it, Mattie?"

She backed slowly off from him, a step at a time. "No. You want to dicker, it's his life for the gold. And I ain't part of the bargain."

Riordan moved forward, matching her retreat step for step. His eyes narrowed to pale slits in the shadow of the hat. "You don't get it, honey girl. I ain't asking you, I'm telling. You'll go along with my idee or I put a bullet in him right now. Then I will take what I goddamn please anyways and you will be like to get busted up something awful. It don't need to be that way."

Riordan had moved past Carrighar, who lay behind him and a little to his right now. From the tail of her eye, Mattie caught a flash of shining metal. She dared one flicking glance at Carrighar. He had moved, the sun flashing off his big belt buckle.

Riordan said, "Well, girl? What you say?"

She held her gaze square on Riordan's face as Carrighar, holding onto the rock, dragged himself slowly and quietly to his feet. Then he was hobbling with a terrible dogged energy toward Riordan's back, half dragging his bad leg to keep it from crumpling under him. His teeth were bared; blood streamed down his face from his scalp.

Something in Mattie's expression, or maybe a whisper of sound, warned Riordan. He whirled around, the rifle swinging in a fast arc.

Carrighar dived the last few feet, one arm sweeping the rifle barrel aside. Then, as his bad leg gave way, he drove full-tilt into Riordan, catching him around the waist in an effort to drag him down. Frantically, savagely, Riordan slammed the rifle butt at Carrighar's skull, connecting solidly. It broke Carrighar's hold, dropping him face down in the sand.

Riordan stepped back, levering the rifle.

In the same instant Mattie ran at his back, arms straight out and braced, palms spread; her full weight slammed into the man and sent him reeling, fighting for balance. And then Mattie spun toward Carrighar's .44, just feet away. She scooped it into her hand and came up and around as Riordan recovered his balance, turning, whirling to face her with a snarl as she fired.

The slug's impact flung him backward, his rifle blasting at the sky. But it was a reflex trigger-pull, a last spasm of contracting muscle. When he went down, he didn't move again.

Somehow she was sitting on the ground in Carrighar's arms, shaking wildly and holding him as if she'd never let go. He was talking in a weary, quiet voice, trying to still her trembling.

"We're a fine-looking pair, you know? All bloodied to hell, the both. If you can make shift to stand, girl, and lend me your shoulder, we will get cleaned up some."

When she had eased him down on her father's cot, Mattie set to cutting open the leg of his pants and washing the wound. The bullet had passed clear through the big outer muscle without touching bone or nerve. Carrighar took several long pulls at her pa's jug, letting the wound bleed clean awhile, and then he directed her to heat a knife and close both openings. He made her take a nip from the jug too; then, her nerve steeled and her hand steady, she did a quick, neat job of cauterizing the wound. Carrighar didn't let out a sound, and then he passed out quietly while she was bandaging his leg.

Mattie sat and watched him as he slept, her face very gentle with her thoughts. After a time she got up and fetched the shovel, and began digging a straight-down hole in the northeast corner of the shack's dirt floor. Shortly she was on her knees, lifting one small heavy canvas sack after another out of the hole, piling them beside her till there were a dozen in all.

It was dusk when Carrighar groggily awoke. He stirred, grimaced, and blinked at the lamp light, then at Mattie Ingersol and the row of bulging canvas sacks on the table.

"There it is," she said quietly. "What you and Jack wanted to see so bad. That's my pa's cache."

"But——"

"It's ours now. Mine and yours. I changed my mind. A woman can change her mind. I am going with you, Les."

He was silent, digesting her words, and then he studied her serene face for a time. "All right," he said at last. "You and me and the gold. That's how it'll be. But we ain't going for Mexico. Our way's north."

"North," she whispered. "But where?"

"You're going to my brother's place. Him and his wife

got a little ranch up in the Squaw Peak country. You're going to 'em with a letter from me. It'll tell all they need to know."

"But what about you?"

"You will be dropping me off on the way—at Yuma Prison." He scowled, as if fumbling for words now. "You said it and I know it's so. You ain't a woman to spend her life with a man's got to keep looking over his shoulder. Don't reckon I got belly for it myself."

"Have you any belly for that place?"

"Not much, Mattie girl, not much." He grinned that small, crooked grin. "But I go back now and give myself up, I might not have to serve more'n two, three more years, at the most. And that gold of ours can hire a good lawyer, maybe get my case appealed to the territorial court."

She came to kneel by the cot, listening, wondering.

"Meantime I'll know you're well cared for. My brother's a good man; his wife is a sweet, kindly woman. They ain't got much money, but they got something a hell of a lot better going in their lives."

He paused, almost shyly. "That feeling you talked about? I reckon we got it and to spare. But there's got to be more, something as good as they got. And this here's the only way we can have that. Mattie, all I want to know now is will you go to them?"

She knew how it would be with the time ahead, the dark time of waiting. And knowing, wanted it no other way.

"I'll go there," she said. "I'll *be* there, Les."

A KIND OF COURAGE

The two men prowled single file along the old game trail where it followed the creek-bank, going upstream. They were young men; both were pared down to bone and muscle. They wore rawhide moccasins and leggings of colored stroud, and they had removed their calico shirts against the simmering mid-July heat. They were armed with hickory bows and quivers of arrows, and each carried a steel-headed tomahawk and a scalping knife. Sweat glistened on the coppery skin of their plucked scalps, bare except for the gaudy scalp locks they wore as Sac warriors.

In these ways the two were alike; otherwise they only differed. Their sorry diet had thinned them both almost to the point of emaciation, but the man who walked behind was still heavily muscled. Marked by traces of white war paint, his face was craggy and handsome and held a lurking mischief. He was watchful, his eyes darting swift glances at the surrounding brush.

The youth in the lead was lighter of build, and he wasn't big. His eyes were quiet and withdrawn; deep and questing moods glided like quick fish beneath the surface of his face.

The wind made a hushing sound through the thick

boughs of white pine arching over them. A drift of pine needles, yellowed and dropping in the summer heat, whispered down through the dusty shafts of sunlight. These were the only sounds, for the two Sacs made none—until the man in the rear suddenly struck his bow against a pine trunk.

The noise was sharp and loud in the quivering, sodden air. Tyeema jerked at the sound, then looked back across his shoulder to see the lazy mockery in his companion's face.

Musketabah said sleepily, "One time soon maybe you'll dream yourself into a bird and fly away, and my sister will have no husband."

Tyeema set his face ahead again. There was sweat between his hand and his bow, and he could hear his heart. He was angry at himself for starting at the deliberate noise. Musketabah thought that such tricks were funny.

"Or maybe," Musketabah went on, "you will change into a rabbit. You jump like a rabbit."

Tyeema didn't answer.

"You should have gone with Keokuk and the other women."

"Keokuk is no woman."

"He is an old woman, and so are his friends."

Musketabah's words were soft and very lazy. But the laziness was only a manner he affected, for he missed nothing at all. Musketabah, after all, wasn't given to dangerous dreaming. His mind was so disciplined that it never strayed by a hair's width from the business at hand.

Maybe this was the way to be at such a time, Tyeema thought, letting his anger turn inward.

The gifts for war did not touch each man in like degree. Some had the stronger arms, the sharper eyes, the quicker brains. Tyeema had never come close to equaling his brother-in-law in any game with lance or bow or in the stalk and kill or in wrestling skills. But then few could outstrip Musketabah in any art of hunting or fighting, and he excelled without half trying. Yet his easy, good-natured arrogance sat him so lightly that hardly anybody resented it.

Tyeema, on the other hand, was a rather ordinary fellow as Sac braves went, except in one way—and it was not a good way in such times as these. Tyeema was given to dreaming, not a commendable trait when all a man's senses and thinking should be directed toward two things only—some sign of the white enemy or a sight of the game that was desperately needed to swell the shrunken bellies of the Rock River people.

There had been a scarcity of game since early spring when they had followed Black Hawk across the Mississippi, returning to Senisepo Kebesaukee, their ancestral homeland at the mouth of the Rock River. One bad treaty after another, signed by one weak and ignorant leader after another, had deprived the Sacs of all their former lands east of the Father of Waters. It was old Black Hawk, a mere headman of the Rock River Sacs who, at long last, in this white man's year of 1832, had rebelled against the westward-creeping dominion of the whites. He would bring his people back to their old grounds and plant corn in the old way; he did not want trouble with the Americans, but he would not abide by a bad treaty.

Nobody had argued the truth of Black Hawk's words, but the cooler heads among the Sacs knew that his action was no part of wisdom. The Americans were too strong. The Potawatomi and Winnebagos and Chippewas on this side of the big river had their share of grievances against the whites, but they could spare only half-hearted sympathy for their Sac brothers.

Hoh-hoh—this was a fool's business Black Hawk had started. Surely the British fathers in Canada had encouraged the old man in his foolishness, but why had he thought they would give him active help? Twenty years ago the British and their Indian allies had been unable to seize this land they called the Northwest Territory from the Americans, and today the Americans were even stronger. Yes, Black Hawk was a *poshi-poshito*, a fool of fools, for even his friend Shabonna, the Potawatomi chief, had tried to dissuade him and, failing that, had gone so far as to warn the soldiers and settlers of Black Hawk's intentions.

As to the Sacs themselves, many remained loyal to Keokuk, chief of their nation, a man whose bitterness toward the whites he had once befriended was tempered by an acid fatalism. He had made the best terms that could be made with the Americans, and hotheads like Black Hawk and his ill-advised counselors, Neapope and The Prophet, would only bring down the white man's wrath on all the Sacs.

Tyeema knew these things, and the folly of this war had been strong in his thoughts long before Black Hawk had made his move. Since he was not of the Rock River tribe and owed them no allegiance, why had he stayed? There was an easy answer: he had married a Rock River woman and had come into her family, according to custom. His wife's father and brother had red war in their minds, and what the women thought did not matter. So they had stayed with Black Hawk, and so had Tyeema.

That was the easy answer, but there was more to Tyeema's decision than that. At first it had seemed important to change that lazy contempt in Musketabah's eyes, a thing that had long made a great knot in Tyeema's guts. If he weren't a great fighter or hunter, still he was not a fool or a cripple; he could be as brave as the next man.

The trouble was that Tyeema *was* afraid, and Musketabah knew it. No matter how often Tyeema told himself that his brother-in-law's cool, easy mockery of him should not matter, did not matter, the sting of shame was still left festering in him. Staying with Black Hawk had been a mistake, but all he could do now was keep silent and swallow what he must until Black Hawk's great folly reached a bloody end.

Three and a half months ago, when the Sacs had crossed the Mississippi at the Yellow Banks, there had been a prompt reaction from Reynolds, the white chief of Illinois, and from the White Beaver, General Atkinson of the American garrison at Fort Armstrong. In no time at all fully five thousand regular troops and Illinois militiamen were in the field, picking up the trail of half a thousand Sac warriors and their families. Even Black Hawk, the old fire-eater, had quickly seen the wisdom of a parley. But when a company of militia led by a capering white fool called Stillman had fired on and killed the emissaries sent by Black Hawk under a truce flag, the enraged chief had slaughtered and routed the whole gang, though his party was outnumbered three to one.

Then and afterward, Black Hawk had proved himself an able and wily leader. Swiftly retreating, he and his Sacs were swallowed by the wilderness. Though burdened by their women and children and their animals and belongings, the Rock River people had eluded the white patrols for many weeks. All the while the Sacs were forging steadily northward toward the bluffs of the Wisconsin River and their final stand, throwing out a swift flurry of raids among the scattered, helpless settlers.

Black Hawk had made an amazing fight—even Tyeema had to admit as much—but in the end it would all be the same. If the whites were paying a terrible price, the misery of the Sacs was three times as great as theirs. Not in the worst winters recalled by the elders had the people been reduced to the state of near-starvation that now threatened them, thanks to long marches, short sleeps, and whatever snatches of food they could find or take from the whites.

It was not enough. The people were wasting to tottering skeletons. Some were too weak to continue the march; several had already died. All the horses that could be spared had been eaten. Since all food was shared alike, all were now living mainly on a little cracked corn, acorns, elm bark—even grass.

In a valley to the north, the main band was resting over a day; this made a little time for the men to hunt. Maybe Gitchee-Manitou would smile today. Tyeema, thinking of his wife's hollow-eyed face, hoped it might be so. Even a scrawny rabbit would be welcome in the pot. Nan-nah-que, the father, was too sick and weak to go with them, so Tyeema and Musketabah were prowling the stream-banks alone.

There was no wind near the ground; the air was heavy with the wet heat of noonday. The sluggish creek flickered with green-gold rays of sunlight. Tyeema thought he was seeing all there was to be seen—the static burring of a dragonfly above the water, the knotlike lump of a mud turtle on a half-sunk log, a slim green snake gliding away through the dry cattails. But suddenly Musketabah was at his side, gripping his wrist and pointing through the trees.

There was movement on the creek-bank well upstream, a transient spot of color had showed and moved and was gone. That was all, and the two Sacs froze to the spot. When they eased cautiously forward once more, Musketabah brushed Tyeema aside and took the lead.

Soon the voices and words of white men reached them. The camp came into view on the opposite side of the creek. It was set back off the bank, in the trees. There was a rattle of coarse laughter. Tyeema smelled a pine wood fire and roasting meat; his belly ached sorely, and his saliva started to work on nothing.

The two Sacs crept close to the water's edge, for the reeds and willow brush hid them, and they were still many yards downstream from the camp. They watched awhile but could make out little because of the trees.

Musketabah murmured, "These Long Knives are a war party, but they are not dressed like the soldiers. How are they called?"

"Militia." The white man's word rolled easily off Tyeema's tongue.

"Mil-lish-ah." Musketabah grunted contemptuously. "Maybe we'll find out how much of a rabbit you are." He peered tightly through the water reeds. "We will go under the water to the other side. That log—there—will hide us. Then we'll be close enough."

"Close enough for what?" Tyeema's heart began a dense, almost painful slugging against his ribs.

"To hear what they say, fool. You've gone to the post

school at Prairie du Chien; you know their foolish language. Maybe you've also taken a white man's watery heart in your guts; we'll learn about that too."

Tyeema said, "What does my brother mean?" though he knew the answer well enough. The spittle had dried on his tongue.

"There will be danger. That close, if we are seen, we won't have time to get away before we're killed or captured." Musketabah's whisper was light. "How brave does my brother feel?"

"It is a foolishness," Tyeema said coldly. "If these Americans are so close to our camp, maybe they'll cross our trail soon. Then they'll find where we are and send word to the White Beaver, and he will bring up troops. The Sacs are not ready to meet the soldiers here. We should go tell Black Hawk to break camp at once and go north swiftly."

"Yes, rabbit, but first we will learn of this mil-lish-ah's plans if we can. That's only wisdom."

It was stupidity, Tyeema knew. The only wisdom was to backtrack as quickly as possible; Black Hawk would want to know at once of a large company of well-armed whites this close to his main camp. If Musketabah wanted to take a senseless risk, that was his business.

Even as the thought formed, so did the one bleak flaw in it: Tyeema's own weakness.

He could tolerate no more of Musketabah's taunting charges of cowardice. And if he deserted him now, no matter that his was the wise action, the contempt that only Musketabah had shown would be shared by his wife's family and by many others in the band. Since he really was afraid, he could not be sure just how much the fear was affecting his judgment. How could a man leave such a question unanswered and face himself in the night?

He did not show Musketabah another twinge of reluctance; he said only, "I can do this alone. While I remain to hear what the white men say, let Musketabah go without delay to warn Black Hawk."

Musketabah's eyes slitted; the suggestion had obviously touched his pride. "Since when does one trust a rabbit to carry through a man's work?" His whisper was very soft and flat. "I'll see that you do it well. Follow a man, rabbit."

Without another word he slipped off his quiver and laid it aside with his bow, then crept forward through the reeds and slid noiselessly into the creek. Tyeema did not let himself think. He discarded his bow and arrows, then followed his brother-in-law. The water was warm as he went under, but he felt the instant chilly drag of the current at his legs. Underwater, he opened his eyes and saw Musketabah stroking his way upstream through a golden flood of sunlight.

Tyeema moved after him. A string of bubbles tickled up past his cheeks and ears. A school of minnows, swarming past like brown darts, nibbled along his shoulders and arms. His lungs were starting to burst. He saw Musketabah swing close to the bank and paddle to the surface.

Fighting the instinct to claw blindly up to air, Tyeema forced himself to break surface lightly, with a faint, neat rustle of water. Then he had to fight to keep from gulping the air, taking it in, instead, in shuddering, shallow gasps.

Close beside him, Musketabah laughed silently.

They were hugging the side of a huge deadfall by the

bank; they treaded water, their heads hidden by the rotted trunk. A greenish scum of alga lapped at their chins. Tyeema's heart was pounding more furiously than ever; the weakness of pure hunger had made that brief underwater swim an agonizing effort. Musketabah showed no sign of exertion.

"And then she said, 'Well, I'll be a son of a bitch!'" one of the white rangers said loudly and clearly.

Several of the others laughed. There was a group of them sitting toward this side of the camp, telling stories. Tyeema knew the kind, these being white militia.

He was surprised how easy it was to make out their individual words now. They were still a fair distance away, as the two Sacs could tell by raising themselves till their eyes just topped the log. Tall reeds grew on the creek-bank, and beyond it tall grasses and a few birches grew up to the edge of the bivouac. They could make out enough to tell that this was a good sized company. A large number of rangers were squatting or lying on their backs around a clearing, talking and resting. The several fires were smoking less than most white men's fires. These were a rough and seasoned-looking lot in worn homespuns and buckskins, all of them bearded from many days in the wilderness. But the camp was well-ordered and clean; it was clear there was discipline here.

Tyeema took particular notice of three men standing near the center of the camp. Two of them were obviously guides and scouts: one, a métis, wore cast-off white man's clothes, the other, a full-blood, wore the regalia of a Winnebago chief. The third was a tall white man in a fringed hunting coat; he appeared to be the leader. His yellow beard chopped slowly up and down as he talked.

WESTWARD THEY RODE

In answer to a question, the Winnebago, a middle-aged man with a lined and wolfish face, pointed toward the north.

Musketabah murmured close to Tyeema's ear, "I want to hear what that yellow beard says. I'll get closer."

Tyeema wanted to call him a fool. "If you get closer, you'll be seen."

"Are these mil-lish-ah different from other whites? Their senses are dead in the woods."

"The Winnebago's senses aren't dead."

"I don't ask you to come, rabbit," Musketabah whispered.

He slithered around the log and crawled from the water past the red-covered bank. Noiseless as a shadow, he snaked on his belly through the tall grass, which stirred in a slight graceful motion that the mild wind covered.

Suddenly Musketabah halted; his arm whipped up and back. His tomahawk flashed and fell. Tyeema had a glimpse of the huge bull snake, headless now, thrashing in the grass.

The hearty noise and activity of the whites should have hidden the spare sound and movement Musketabah had made killing the snake, but the Winnebago's head promptly turned, his eyes pouncing through the birches and the tall grass. He was leaning on his Kentucky rifle, and now he brought up the long-barreled piece and started across the clearing.

Musketabah knew the game was up. He was on his feet at once, wheeling back toward the creek in a low, darting run. The Winnebago's rifle made a sharp, ringing report, and Musketabah was knocked down, then went somersaulting onto his back. He staggered to his feet but almost fell again. By then the militiamen were coming on the run, the yellow beard yelling, "I want that reddie alive!"

Musketabah stumbled on, but the métis and three white men were almost at his heels. He swung on them, tomahawk lifted. His arm whipped forward; the war ax made a turning flash of steel that ended in the chest of a white man. He had no time to get out his knife then, as the métis and the other two whites swarmed into Musketabah and carried him to the ground while he fought like a wounded black bear.

Tyeema stayed where he was, not moving a muscle. If he remained absolutely still, the log and heavy growth of reeds would hide him from anything but a close search.

The rest of the whites came up as the three men were wrestling Musketabah to his feet. "*Sacre bleu*," the métis panted. "This one, he is fight like ten t'ousan' devil." The others gathered around the one who was dead in the grass with the tomahawk in his chest; there was a run of ominous talk.

The leader tugged his yellow beard, eying Musketabah. "Well, here's a piece of luck."

"Not so lucky for George," a man growled.

"I mean taking the hostile alive. This 'un has to be a scout for Black Hawk. We was pretty sure the main band wasn't far from here. This seems to prove it. Walking Thunder!"

The Winnebago finished methodically loading and priming his rifle before moving over to the leader.

"I want to know some things. Where the main band is, what its strength is, and what this fellow knows of Black Hawk's plans."

Walking Thunder spoke a few sentences in the Sac tongue to Musketabah, who did not even look at him. "He not talk now," the Winnebago reported to the yellow beard. "You give him me, I take him in woods. By and by, he talk."

"I say gut the bastard here and now, Cap'n," a man said softly. "He killed a white man. It's a white man's job."

There was a general clamor of agreement, put down harshly by the captain. "I know how you feel. But any information we can coax out o' him comes first. You boys'll have what's left o' him, you can lay to that."

"My God, Captain Macready." A beardless young man had spoken up, his voice full of shock. "This is barbarous! You're not actually turning a wounded captive over to this savage?"

"It's their way, boy. They lived by it a long time. I don't aim to preach 'em no different. And we need what this reddie can tell us."

"But you are a white man, sir, and you're permitting this—this dastardly——"

"Listen, sonny." Captain Macready's eyes held a blue glitter. "Some of Black Hawk's bunch got my brother and his family a month back. They skinned my brother alive and left him in the sun. There's plenty men here had things as bad touch them and theirs. You want to ask someone any more about it, here's your chance."

The young man said nothing.

"Maybe a hundred white lives'll be saved if we can run Black Hawk to ground now," Captain Macready went on. "Once we know what we need to, we'll send a runner back to General Henry, and him and Colonel Dodge'll bring their troops up double-quick. I don't aim to abuse no tender ears, so we'll take the redskin off a ways. Walking Thunder, Doucette—lay hold of him. Rest of you get about your business."

The Winnebago and the métis caught Musketabah by the arms. His head had dropped to his chest; he was bleeding badly, and for the moment the fight seemed to have run out of him.

Captain Macready turned and led the way into the dense pine woods along the creek, followed by the two men supporting the wounded Sac between them. The militiamen were strangely silent, not meeting one another's eyes, as they picked up their dead comrade and carried him back to the camp.

Tyeema waited till they had all cleared away from the area by the bank; even then he didn't move quickly as he pulled himself on his belly from the water.

He was undecided.

It was more urgent than before that Black Hawk be warned promptly, for even if Musketabah died without talking, the militia were now sure that the Sac encampment was close by; they would scour the region for it.

But there was Musketabah.

And suddenly Tyeema quit wondering. Lying flat in the grass, he inched forward into the pines until the forest blocked him from the camp. Then he climbed to his feet and fell into a light jog-trot, heading through the woods along the creek on the trail taken by the militia captain.

He was a fool, Tyeema supposed. He had no great affection for his brother-in-law, and his were not the gifts of war. Even if he weren't almost staggering with the weakness of hunger, even if he had the bow and arrows he had left back on the other bank, he would stand little chance against the long rifles of Macready and Walking Thunder, or even the ancient Hudson Bay musket that Doucette carried. If there were only one instead of three, and if he had a bow or gun, and if he could take the men by surprise . . . but there he was, dreaming. He had none of these advantages, all he had was a bad habit of indulging in idle speculation.

Then a faint excitement touched Tyeema, quickening his step a little. At least one of his ideas might have some meat to it. The realization didn't surprise him; just as courage and physical skills came hard to him, so ideas came easily. He turned this one over briefly in his mind and thought it was sound. Musketabah, he knew, would be expecting nothing from him in the way of help, and that knowledge tightened his belly. Tyeema decided to try his plan before he lost his nerve.

His senses were quickening now; at last he heard the faint lift of voices that told him the men he was following had stopped not far ahead. Tyeema halted and squatted, digging his fingers into the forest loam. With a handful of gritty soil, he scrubbed away the traces of white war paint on his body; he smeared the moist dirt on his skin and then rubbed it on his breechclout and leggings. He trimmed the feathers and porcupine quills from his ornate scalp lock with his knife, leaving a ragged tuft of hair.

When these things were done, Tyeema cut a sorry figure that nobody would take for a Sac warrior. He was even forced to discard his tomahawk, for although it was a useful weapon, it would also clash with the picture he wanted to make. He would have to rely on his knife alone, and cached the tomahawk in the crotch of a tree. He partly circled the small cut of clearing to which the militia captain and the other two had brought Musketabah; he wanted to come on it from a direction that would arouse the least suspicion.

He dropped into a languid shuffle, his muscles loose and his mouth pulled into a vacant grin, as he came slowly out of the woods into the clearing.

Walking Thunder saw him first. He also saw at once what Tyeema had relied on him to see. The Winnebago's lips began to move in an uneasy and soundless chant; he kept watching Tyeema. The métis was sitting on his haunches, striking flint and steel to make a fire. He glanced up; his eyes narrowed. "*Grace a Dieu,*" he muttered.

Captain Macready was keeping his eyes on Musketabah, who was sitting on the ground, one fist clamped over his shoulder muscle above the bleeding. At Doucette's low mutter, the captain looked around. He gave an oath and started to swing his rifle up. Walking Thunder threw out a long arm and said a flat, chopping phrase. Macready paused, looking at Doucette.

"What'd he say?"

"Bad—bad to kill." Doucette tapped his head, then stabbed a finger at Tyeema. "Walking Thunder say is bad spirit in this one's head."

Tyeema halted and rolled his eyes from one man to the next, grinning idiotically.

Captain Macready stared at him for a long suspicious moment. "All right, what of it? Looks Sac to me. Loony Injuns are as bad as any kind. Maybe worse."

"*Non*—you don' comprehen', *Capitaine*. This one, he is touch' in the head by Gitchee-Manitou—he is ver' holy. He is no more of his people; they have turn' him out. Bad luck to kill—big bad luck."

"The hell." Macready was scowling, but he lowered his rifle a little. "You believe that?"

"*Non*, not Doucette." The métis laughed, but Tyeema sensed that he was afraid.

Grinning, Tyeema walked slowly into the clearing now, reserving a glance for Musketabah. His brother-in-law was eying him with openmouthed amazement, and Tyeema only hoped he would stay that way and show nothing else.

Tyeema rubbed his belly as he shuffled over to the half-breed. "Food—food."

"Ha, w'at you t'ink? He's hungry, this one." Doucette gave another nervous laugh; he watched with fearful fascination as Tyeema's hand came up to his shoulder.

Tyeema laughed childishly, patting the métis's shoulder. "Food—food. Friend. You give food."

Captain Macready began to grin. His hands relaxed, letting his Kentucky flintlock slip down through his fingers till the butt touched the ground. "He 'pears to of took a liking to you, Doucette." He was enjoying this now.

"Ha ha," said Doucette. He patted the Sac's shoulder. "What is my brother's name? Eh? Name?"

Tyeema rubbed his belly and said vapidly, "Strawberry," since his name meant that in English. "Strawberry want food."

"Ho, ho! M'sieu Strawberry!" Doucette laughed loudly, turning his head to wink at the captain. "Strawberry! That is a good name for the loony Injun, eh, *Capitaine?* Strawb—"

The last word was choked off in a gurgling shriek as Tyeema, covered by Doucette's body, drove his scalping knife hard and low into the métis' belly, twisting the blade. Doucette leaned into him, his whole body strung in one hard spasm; he was still on his feet, the dying scream trailing in his throat, as Tyeema wrenched the musket from his hands.

Tyeema leaped away from the falling man, at the same time bringing the musket to bear on Walking Thunder rather than the white man. It was well he did, for the Winnebago's reaction was like lightning.

His long rifle was sweeping level even as Tyeema cocked the old musket and shot point-blank, awkwardly, into Walking Thunder's chest. The Winnebago went down, his piece unfired.

In wild haste now, Tyeema spun on his heel to face the white man, both hands clubbed around the empty musket. But Musketabah, as he had hoped, had leaped with his expected quickness. Sitting on the ground, quite close to Captain Macready, he had simply lunged sideways and yanked the white man's feet from under him, then grappled him.

Musketabah had a death grip on the man. Musketabah brought Macready's rifle across the white man's throat, and pressed down on the windpipe, crushing it. Captain Macready's mouth sagged open, but he was still fumbling along his belt for his hunting knife. Tyeema got there first and pulled the knife from its sheath and plunged it into the militia captain's heart.

Musketabah rolled the dead man aside and got to his feet. The others would be coming fast; the musket shot would bring them, Tyeema pointed out, and there was no time to lose.

That didn't trouble Musketabah. The Winnebago was still alive, and Musketabah took the time to remedy that detail. He also took the time to arm himself with Macready's knife, his rifle, powder horn, and shot pouch. He insisted that Tyeema take the Winnebago's rifle and accouterments.

"Where is your tomahawk?" he asked.

Wordlessly, resignedly, Tyeema pointed at the woods, and Musketabah said, "We'll get it. Then go across the creek for our bows and quivers." He slapped Tyeema's shoulder. "You were a smart rabbit to leave the tomahawk before you did your little trick. Even a rabbit can have good brains. Come!"

Less than a minute later, after they had left the clearing, retrieved the tomahawk, and were starting for the creek, a hubbub of men's angry voices came from the clearing. There wasn't fifty yards of forest between the clearing and the two Sacs as Musketabah plunged into the water, but he was in no particular hurry. On the other side he paused to plaster his wound with mud, then held Tyeema down to his own leisurely arrogant trot as they went back to where they had left their bows and arrows.

The tightness in Tyeema's belly did not ease till they were a mile from the creek, moving back in an idle circle toward the main camp, for Musketabah still hoped to scare up some game.

Soon they flushed a pair of lean rabbits from the brush, and Musketabah knocked one over with an arrow. Tyeema missed his shot.

"You should practice with the rifle," Musketabah told him, scooping up the dead rabbit. "With it, you might do better. Unless the noise will frighten you too greatly."

Tyeema had been staring moodily at the ground, but his patience snapped then. He turned on Musketabah, rage in his heart, and then saw that Musketabah was grinning at him in a lazy, arrogant, and wholly engaging way.

Musketabah swung the dead rabbit by the ears. "Well," he said critically, "no brother of this one could have helped me count coup on three enemies. That took a kind of courage, I suppose. Yes, and you have good brains, Tyeema. But you're slow as a turtle. Why, that old Winnebago almost killed you, and if Musketabah hadn't been there, the white man would have gotten you instead."

"Yes," Tyeema said. "But——"

"And you missed your rabbit," Musketabah added with satisfaction.

What was the use? "Yes," said Tyeema, "and by the length of a tall man's arm."

"I thought so," Musketabah said agreeably. "But my brother will have a share of my kill."

ONE FOR THE MONEY

After I'd finished cleaning out the stalls of Titus Davies' livery barn, I went to lean in the barn's front archway and roll my cigarette for the morning, careful not to spill any tobacco. I returned the thin bag of Durham to my shirt pocket and lighted up while I gave the main street of Caprock a look-over. A double row of false-fronted buildings flanking a dusty street. Caprock hardly looked any different from when I'd first clapped eyes on it a year ago.

The town had mushroomed to life pretty much the way any Kansas railhead town had after track reached it, making it a new and better point from which to ship Texas cattle to the packing houses in Kansas City and Chicago. On the heels of bawling herds of stringy-muscled longhorns came trail hands thirsty for a whoop-up at trail's end. They had been preceded by the usual crowd of gamblers, saloonmen and camp women who'd followed the rail-builders. Of course the place had attracted a passel of tough-nut sorts, but also a handful of solid folk-looking to stay and invest and build had come as well.

Now at summer's end, still in off season, Caprock resembled nothing livelier than a tired dog sprawled in the sun. Here on the rolling Kansas prairie, the name of the place didn't apply too well. The town had been dubbed Caprock by the Texas drovers who'd pushed the first-arriving herds clear from the red wastes of the Texas caprock. I was thinking about that, and about the future—the town's and my own—when Titus Davies came tramping down the street to open his office for the day.

The livery owner hauled up in front of me and scowled, teetering back and forth on his heels. He was a round-bellied little man who most of the time wore a glowering and growly manner, maybe to defy what all folks say about fat men being jolly. But you couldn't find a better boss to work for.

"Always the early bird, huh, Sam? You had breakfast yet?"

"No, sir. Wanted to get the stable in good order first. Man's *got* to get up early to keep ahead of the game."

"That's right, world-beater," Mr. Davies grunted. "Well, I got a piece of news should help your digestion. Or raise all sorts of hob with it. Town council was in late session last night, making the choice of a new city marshal."

"I reckon it's time, with the first drovers about due."

"Uh-huh. Did you reckon they might vote unanimously to give you the job?"

"What?"

"That's what they went and done, bub."

I dropped my cigarette in pure surprise, then gave it a quick unthinking scuff with my heel. I expect I gawked like a kid, for Mr. Davies showed a flinty streak of teeth, his version of a grin. After I was sure my voice would come steady, I said carefully, "You wouldn't josh me, sir, would you?"

"Might, but I ain't. They asked me to carry you the good word, along with this here."

Mr. Davies pulled a battered disc of metal from his coat pocket and held it out. It was the badge Arch Benteen had worn for two years. I took it automatically, my head swimming, fumbled and nearly dropped it before I got it pinned to my vest, kind of straightening up as I did so, feeling the instant responsibility that went with it.

"I'm mighty honored, sir. Thank you."

"You are thanking the wrong councilman," Mr. Davies growled. "It was Kyle Garth brought up your name while we was debating possibilities. He pointed out you're absolutely steady, a hard worker, never drink, and are a model of efficiency at anything you turn your hand to. Hell, he didn't need to convince me. I call the suggestion sort of inspired, considering the source."

Kyle Garth? Well, I couldn't quite tie that.

As owner of half of Caprock's gaming and watering holes where fresh-in-town Texans washed down the dust and wasted their hard-earned pay, Kyle Garth commanded respect, but you'd never say an excess of social intimacy, with the more solid citizens. They'd only reluctantly and recently granted him a seat on the town council.

"Surprised me, too," Mr. Davies observed dryly, "Garth turning out a big head of civic responsibility so almighty sudden, particular where a peace officer is concerned. Wa'n't no love lost between him and Arch Benteen, you know. Arch rode a helluva tight rein on the casinos and saloons, including Garth's."

I fingered the badge. It was still hard to keep my hands off it. "I surely hope I can meet expectations, sir."

"So do I. Don't think there wasn't some objections raised along with your name. Ham Byers and Tim O'Mara, well, they agreed Sam Hartley was an upcoming young fellow and all, but your tender years bothered 'em. Me, I allowed twenty-two ain't any too ripe, but pointed out you ain't altogether green to the work. You served Arch as a special deputy off and on. You're big enough, fast on your feet, a dead shot, and damn handy with your fists if some lunkhead pushes you to it."

It was a lot of praise from Mr. Davies, so much that he cut himself short and kind of glared at me. "Besides which," he said testily, "they wa'n't a whole helluva lot of options open to us. Practically narrowed down to the one man in this damn place under thirty-five who's got brains and guts in one package and ain't a rummy. Old Wylie Connell made that point, and him and me and Garth swung the other two into making it unanimous." He paused, giving his nose a tug, and added, "Don't you fool yourself none. You got a tough ax to grind and some big boots to fill. Never forget that a mighty good man wore that badge."

I gave a sober nod; I knew it. In his time Arch Benteen had helped tame some of the meanest of trail towns. That's why, after the Pacific Southwest Railroad had created Caprock—which grew up around Mud Creek, an old station on the Haines and Harmer Stage Line—the town founders had invited Arch Benteen to police their town. His head might have been gray, but his nerve was still sound, his eye keen, his hand steady; he'd done handily at keeping the wildest of those Texas tough-hands in line. Until last Saturday night, when he was killed trying to break up a drunken brawl.

It brought to mind something Arch Benteen had once told me. *When a man risks his neck in a job, he better be sure he is getting his worth from it.* A good thought, that.

I pulled up my shoulders and looked Mr. Davies square in the eye. "About the pay, sir. . . ."

"Yeh," he grunted dryly. "I allowed you wouldn't be slow to raise *that* point, Sam. You'll get what Arch got, a hundred dollars a month, plus expenses. Includes the pay of a deputy or two or three, as and when you require 'em. I wore out my lip flapping it at the others 'bout how you was worth Arch's pay. You better not let me down."

"You don't need to worry."

"I don't think I do." Mr. Davies gave me a cuff on the arm, saying gruffly, "Go on, get you some breakfast. Reckon you can fetch Bonabeth Connell a nice surprise while you're about it. That's if she don't mind her beau getting into a way where he's like to get his pretty ears notched."

I grinned. "I reckon her daddy has told her."

"Nope. Wylie told me he wants you to have that pleasure. Dunno whether that's good or bad. Here—" He dug in his pocket and hauled out a bunch of keys. "These'll get you into your office, desk and cell block. You are set to go."

I thanked him again and headed down the street toward the Connell Cafe, feeling as lighthearted as a pup in clover. It was a fat stroke of luck to have all this dumped in my lap all of an ordinary morning, and my mind raced across all that it could mean to me.

I had a deep feel for the idea of roots and permanence. I suppose it came from getting orphaned young and raised by an uncle who'd spent my growing-up years roaming the gold fields from California to Colorado, following one will-o'-the-wisp after another. I'd come nineteen when Uncle Mike had died of a bad liver in a lonely mountain cabin, and it had been *me* looking after *him* those last sorry years, after the tanglefoot had got him. It tough-bred a boy, living that way, and left him with a strong taste for better things. I'd worked for different cow outfits before I'd come to Caprock.

If the town followed the usual way of such places, it had two, maybe three more good years as a cattle-shipping point before the Pacific Southwestern was able to finance the building of spur lines to better places. The Panic of '73 had come down hard on the railroads; building had outstripped the needs of a little-settled country. When things picked up again, Caprock's real future would be foretold by settlers from the midwest. Already numbers of them were homesteading or buying up railroad land on the surrounding prairie and bringing in good crops of winter wheat. Caprock, soon to be declared the county seat of Caprock County, faced a bright future as the center of a prosperous farming country. A young fellow who planned and invested wisely could grow with it.

For a year I'd been working hard at a variety of jobs, none of 'em full-time, never tying myself down to one employer or one line of work. I asked for and got good pay for hard work; I'd saved every cent I could and kept my ears open, hoarding up all I could learn about the country, its people and politics, and a goodly know-how for all kinds of business and plain sweat-work. I'd kept myself a free agent, and when the time came I would put my savings and know-how to work for me, starting off strong. I figured to be one of the county's leading citizens before I turned thirty.

The marshal's job would tie down my activities some, but it also meant an early boost in prestige, while that hundred dollars a month was all gravy; I could save every dollar. It was work that would allow me lots of time to pursue my own sidelines and increase my experience. Altogether, it would shave years off reaching my goal.

And it would allow me leisure for a proper courting of Bonabeth Connell. The way I'd been working from dawn to dusk—sweeping out stores, saloons and stables, unpacking and sorting merchandise for merchants, hauling hay for ranchers and farmers in season, breaking and training horse stock for Titus Davies and others—had left precious little time for courting a girl as a man ought. The more menial-style chores would have to go anyway, being below the dignity of a town official.

Bonabeth was a mighty level-headed girl—I liked that most about her—and I figured she understood about me and my goals. For a fact, we'd never discussed the matter a whole lot, but she'd never complained either. All the same she had other suitors—I thought particularly of Will Lundeen—and though I seemed the odds-on favorite, it was high time I got to see more of her. I ought to take her places more often. I'd had to pass up the church social last week because of a horse-breaking job. Tonight, I remembered, there was a dance at the just-built community hall.

Bonabeth was serving coffee to a pair of customers as I pushed through the cafe doors into a steamy gale of breakfast cookery. I took a counter stool by the door, roostering out my chest a little as Bonabeth came down the length of the counter to where I sat. She pushed a straggle of curly black hair off her forehead and flashed her quick good morning grin. Slender and little, she had a wiry strength about her and could muster the same bright grin after a day of slinging grub and taking smart guff from some customers.

"Morning, mister. We're fresh out of everything."

"Even smiles?"

She fetched me another. "Oh, I suppose for a steady customer we can always wrangle an old soup sandwich or something."

"Nice day for something." I gave my badge a casual thumb-nudge. "You reckon it might rain?"

Bonabeth's eyes, a sort of shiny jade color, widened. "Why, look at that. For mercy's sake, Sam."

I accepted her congratulations with a grand nothing-at-all ma'am manner, which I was a little taken aback to see that she appeared to share. The news hadn't brought her up as bright-eyed as I'd hoped. Hiding my disappointment, I gave her my order and waited impatiently while she passed it to the Chinese cook. As she poured a cup of coffee and set it before me, I cleared my throat.

"There's the community dance tonight. You want to go?"

She set the coffee carefully before me. "You do have a sweet way of asking. I almost hate to say no."

"Huh? Did Will already ask you?"

"Two days ago, Sam."

Seems whenever a body is feeling rocket-high, a letdown comes all the faster and harder. Right now I felt a green-eyed cut clear to my innards.

Will Lundeen was an easy fellow to like. His pa had been one of the town founders, owner of three stores, the feed company and the hotel. He'd also bought up hundreds of acres of railroad land cheap when the Pacific Southwestern had unloaded a passel of the federal grant sections along its right of way during the Panic, land the value of which as farm acreage had suddenly zoomed. The old man's recent death had left young Will the country's biggest landholder and one of its up-and-coming wealthy, a fact that didn't hurt his popularity a lick. I hadn't grudged Will his good fortune—even if he'd never had to work a day for it—till right this minute.

"I don't reckon he was the only one who asked."

Bonabeth gave me a cool eye. "No, not the only one. Frank Hubbard and Merl Kinsley asked me to the dance too, if you have to know."

"But it's Will, huh?"

"I think I know how you're thinking, Sam."

"Do you?"

"I only wish I didn't."

"What's that mean, now?"

"This is not the place to discuss it," she said tartly.

I lowered my voice, leaning forward. "Look, my prospects are picking up considerable, and fast too."

"Are they? That's nice. You want some more coffee?"

I pushed away from the counter and stood up. "I don't reckon I'm so hungry after all." I pulled out a coin and slapped it on the counter. "Sorry to of bothered you."

"Sam!"

I felt a high burn of temper rising in me, and knew better than to say more. I turned and walked out, heading for the marshal's office, sharp and dismal thoughts crackling in my head.

It must have been coming up serious between Bonabeth and Will Lundeen a long time, and I'd been too thick to notice it. Well, dammit, if that's how it was, all right, I thought, all right!

My way took me past the Nugget Casino. As I came abreast of it, Kyle Garth was leaning in the doorway in his shirt sleeves, smoking a cigar.

He gave me a civil nod. "Morning, Hartley."

I paused by the steps, not wanting to appear too friendly. "Morning, sir. I hear I owe you a vote of thanks."

Garth, a gaunt-faced man in his late forties, smiled that funny smile of his that never reached his dark, bland eyes. "Nothing to it, boy. I'd say that badge is pinned right where it should be. And you're liable to find it beats all hell out of swamping out my saloons."

For some reason or other that nettled me. "I expect I will."

"Well, I take to heart that good scriptural injunction about casting your bread on the waters. It's a little like spinning the wheel. You never know what may turn up."

"I suppose that's right."

"Sure it is, son. Dame Fortune and the Lord of Hosts work the same side of the street, you mark me." He gave me that bony show-nothing grin again. "Let's have a talk some time, Marshal, all right?"

I nodded and walked on, feeling a shade edgier than before. Bonabeth, now Garth. Seemed people were in a way for dealing riddles today, but I was in no way ready for unraveling them.

I unlocked the marshal's office and went in. The barren brick-walled room contained a battered desk, a couple of chairs, a cot stripped of its blankets, and a gun rack holding two rifles and a Greener shotgun. I tried the keys in the desk drawers and cell doors, finding all the locks in working order. The guns were in working order too, but I'd need a hand weapon. I went through the desk drawers on the off-chance I might find one, but no luck. A good pistol would set me back a good bit, I thought with no enthusiasm. Maybe I could borrow Mr. Davies' gun and save me some money. Anyway I wanted to fetch my plunder from his loft, where I'd been sleeping free.

I walked into his little office at the rear of the livery and said without preliminary, "Mr. Davies, you got a Colt gun in your desk, ain't you?"

"You seen it, Sam."

"Well, I wondered if I might have the loan of it, seeing you never use it."

Grumbling, he took out the holstered Walker Colt wrapped in its shell belt. "You might's well take it. I never been robbed yet, 'cept by Sam Hartley."

"I'm moving my stuff over to the office, sir."

"That's damn good to hear, Sam. It'll help you keep a nice tight fist around all that coin o' yours."

That's three, I thought grimly as I strapped on the gun. I climbed to the loft and threw together my blankets and other gear. When I came down the ladder, two unshaved and sun-blackened men I'd never seen were standing in the archway talking with Mr. Davies. Their looks stamped them as a pair of herders just come off trail.

"So old Arch finally got it, huh? Take a good man to fill his boots."

One of them spoke in a voice that boomed barrel-deep. It fit him; he was built like a hogshead, no taller than Mr. Davies, but with a great spread of shoulders and long powerful arms. He was about sixty, with a good twinkle in his eyes.

"You're just about looking at him," Mr. Davies observed as I left the runway. "Sam Hartley here. Sam, this is Liam Keogh, who they used to call a tough Texan."

I hadn't met Liam Keogh, but had helped Arch Benteen put down a ruckus some of his hands had started last fall.

"Used to, hell," Keogh said amiably. "I can still show any lard-ass counter-jumper like you the what-for, and don't you forget it." He shook hands. "Howdy, son. Ralph Sturges here, my trail boss."

Sturges was a tall, stringy, moody-eyed fellow with a weedy roan mustache. He looked tougher than a roadhouse steak; his bare nod and brief stare-over of me said he wasn't impressed. He moved his feet restlessly, worked his mouth some, spat thinly at the ground. He had some throat-dampening on his mind, I'd bet.

"You coming in to see the elephant, Liam?" Mr. Davies asked.

"Hell, no. I'm too old for that goddamn nonsense. But 'spect my boys will make up for my neglect of the local amenities. They're holding the herd on the river bottom graze while Ralph and I come in to dicker with a buyer. Right now, though, we best find a place to wash the dust down or directly Ralph will be expectorating cotton." Liam Keogh gave me a broad wink. "Keep that badge nice and shiny, son. Makes a hell of a good target."

As the two walked away, Mr. Davies said, "Well, you got a night's work pegged out for you, Sam. Kind of an acid test, you might say. That crew of old Liam Keogh's is the toughest pack of woolly why-hows that ever come up the trail. You keep 'em even halfway in line, you can handle anything this job dishes out. I'd scare up a deputy or two for tonight, I was you."

I thought it over, then shook my head. "No, sir."

"Why not, for hell's sake?"

"Because it's just what you said. A test."

The community hall was lighted up and decorated for the festivities. By six o'clock, the tie rails were lined with wagons and saddle horses. Farmers and crewmen from a handful of outlying ranches could share a social hop of this sort with some mutual toleration. They came through the wide double doors in family groups or couples or singles—self-conscious lads in Sunday best, hair slicked back with tallow; bright-eyed girls in homemade party dresses; older folks looking sedate and reserved. At the door, Wylie Connell checked in the guns of all who wore them, hanging them on wall pegs. I stood beside him, playing it friendly but ready for anything, replying to those who offered me a word of congratulations. I knew everybody and they knew me, and it gave me a high sense of belonging.

Pretty soon Bonabeth and Will Lundeen came in, her hand tucked in his arm, smiling at something he was saying. I thought resentfully that she'd never looked prettier, hair done atop her head and her throat and shoulders bared by the low-cut calico dress she wore. She must have put hours of needlework into readying that dress for tonight. And it had all been for good old Will.

Seeing me, Will let his round face break into a genuine grin. There wasn't a bone of malice in Will's carcass. He extended his hand. "Congratulations, Sam."

That ought to be my word, I thought sourly. "Thanks. Save a dance for me, Bonabeth?"

"Of course." Her smile was reserved, but said she was willing to let bygones be, and I had cooled down sort of fatalistically. There was no sense sulking.

"Sam, I didn't get to say it this morning, but be careful, will you? Just be careful."

"Oh, I'm pretty handy on my feet. Maybe not as handy as some people."

That smart response came out before I could check it, and Bonabeth's trace of warmth dried up. "Then you have no problems, have you? Come along, Will, the music is starting."

A flood of hoofbeats and wild yells sounded down the street from the town's south end. Liam Keogh's crew came barreling into sight. It couldn't be any other; I picked out Ralph Sturges right away. A couple of highbinders careened their ponies, whipping out their hoglegs and emptying them at the sky. Piling out of their saddles, they all headed for the building in a body. My mouth was a shade cottony as I stepped in front of them.

Sturges was in the lead. I caught an aroma of whiskey as he hauled up less than a yard away, looking like he wasn't just ready for trouble, he was inviting it.

"What's in your craw, sonny boy?"

"It's a rule at these affairs to check your guns, Mr. Sturges. You gentlemen wouldn't want to run against the rule, I hope."

Sturges stared at me. "I bet you just hope so!"

Jostling behind their trail boss, the crew fell silent now. Sturges was proddy enough, but not quite sure how green I was—at least that's how I sized him.

I wasn't particularly relieved when he unbuckled his gun belt and passed it to Mr. Connell. I had a gut feeling about Sturges and me, and it was still just the shank of the evening. His men filed in behind him, checking guns and hanging up their hats. You could tell a few of 'em had been nipping, but none to excess—yet. Mr. Connell fetched me a wink; the first round, anyway, was mine.

The fiddlers were jiggling up a varsoviana. The Texas boys took up places in the stag line, nervously slicking back their hair and screwing up their courage to cut in on dancing couples. Already they'd drawn glowering looks from some of the local fellows, but no cause for belly-knots there; neither side would make a ruction with women present.

It was Sturges that I watched.

For a time the trail boss lingered in the stag line, his tar-black eyes cutting across the dancers. It wasn't till Bonabeth and Will Lundeen swept by that Sturges moved suddenly and tapped Will on the shoulder.

"Sorry, brother," Will said pleasantly. "This is a straight number."

He started to waltz Bonabeth away, but Sturges grabbed his arm. I caught Sturges' tight low drawl and an angry retort from Will, but couldn't make out the words. Sturges stared at the younger man with a baiting half-grin that dared him to back whatever he'd said. But Will's eyes fell away; he was ordinarily too pup-friendly, too easy-going, and sure as sin he was no fighter.

Sturges was addressing Bonabeth now. There was consternation in the look she flashed her pa. Wylie Connell's face was grim, but he gave her a faint nod. Let's keep things to a simmer, his look said. Resignedly Bonabeth let Sturges whirl her into the crowd. I got only a glimpse of them for a half a minute or so.

Then I saw that Sturges was holding her too close, and finally he bent his head to whisper in her ear. Bonabeth promptly pulled away and hurried to the door where Will, looking sadly abashed, had joined Mr. Connell and me.

"Will, please take me home."

"What happened?" Will asked lamely.

Mr. Connell's frail form drew up tight as a wire. "Honey, what did he say?"

"Nothing, I just want to go home."

"By God, I've a mind——"

"No, don't. Don't do anything, Dad; it's over. Will?"

Not saying a word, Will took her arm and they went out. Mr. Connell swore softly; I chewed the inside of my lip, watching Sturges swagger back to the stag line. Maybe, if it hadn't been for the smirk he wore, I would have let the matter pass. Maybe not, though, for suddenly I wasn't thinking any more. I walked straight over to where Sturges was leaning against the wall, smirking down at the cigarette he was building.

"I want to see you outside," I told him.

He didn't bother to look up. "Later, kid."

I knocked the makings from his fingers. His right hand dropped to his hip; then he covered the gesture by wiping his palm on his pants. Watching me, hot-eyed, he murmured, "What's eating you, Marshal?"

"Mr. Sturges, you are stepping outside or you are getting dragged out."

"You couldn't drag a shuck, kid, but that's dandy with me."

We headed for the door, where I paused to unfasten my gun belt and hang it up. Then I led the way to a bare lot across the street. About a dozen men who hadn't missed the byplay trailed after us.

They pulled in a half circle about us as we halted in the lot, and I swung a glance around to be sure there was room to square away, but brought my eyes back to Sturges too late. His fist exploded on the point of my jaw. I tried to roll with the punch at the last minute, but my heel hooked on a tuft of grass and down I went.

Sturges was mighty sure of himself, or he'd have jumped on my chest with both feet right then. He just stood there, fists loose at his sides and, oddly, the evil, mocking grin he wore steadied me. Taking it slow, I sat up, my ears ringing but my head clear, sizing him up. Sturges was fast and he was whang-leather-tough; that's all I could be sure of. He was taller'n me, but I shaded him in heft and was about ten years younger. Maybe that would be enough.

I pulled up on my haunches, then came swiftly to my feet, thinking, make him come after you. He moved in, long arms windmilling a flurry of punches. I stepped easily away from the first few and caught another on my arm. When he tried a sledging roundhouse that missed completely and flung him off balance, I stepped in and planted a fist on his mouth.

Sturges let out a howl and bored in on me. I ducked, dodged, backpedaled away from some of his pile drivers and fended most of the rest off my face and body. He was, I judged, used to finishing off an opponent quick and slick with barroom tactics, and I gave him no chance to bring any into play. Even after he began to tire, I continued to easily retreat, pushing only light, careful punches at him. Not a spectacular drubbing, just the kind that'll wear a man down.

Finally he missed a swing that mustered most of his remaining strength and fell against me with a groan. I fired a couple of jabs into his ribs, and as he stepped away, I shifted my body to put weight behind my punch, then slammed a hard right to his chin.

Sturges collapsed on his face, groaned some more, tried to push himself to his knees and failed.

Some locals cheered and slapped me on the back as I pushed through them, going back to the hall for my gun. Afterward I headed for my office, feeling shakily tired myself and sore as a lame bear where Sturges' fists had connected. Titus Davies had been among those watching, and he fell into step alongside me.

"Knew you could handle your dukes, son, but where you learn to prance about and whittle a man down like that? Bastard hardly touched you."

"He touched me enough," I said wryly. "There was an Australian I knew in the gold camps who used to prizefight. He showed me a few tricks."

"Jesus, I guess he did."

"Mr. Davies, I don't reckon it is finished with that man. What do you think?"

"Well, I would call that a discerning thought. Cocky man like Ralph can't of taken a licking very much, and I'd allow never off a badge-toter he had pegged as another wet-eared kid. He is got a reputation with a gun, by the way."

"I didn't know that."

"That's how come I mentioned it, Sam," Mr. Davies said a touch acidly. "What I am saying is Sturges is *damn* good. Killed a couple men in a shoot-out down in Brownsville, Texas, last year and has tipped guns in cattle wars. Don't you ever go up against him with a handgun. You wouldn't stand a beggar's chance."

"What do I do if he braces me?"

Mr. Davies had no answer to that one. It was hard not to stand up to a man on his terms and keep folks' respect, which a lawman needs. I had flung down the gauntlet to Sturges on a personal basis, and he was still the challenged party. If he wanted to carry the matter further. . . .

In the office I stripped off my shirt and gingerly sponged my bruises with cold water. There was still a night's work ahead of me. After the dance broke up, menfolk would be hitting the high spots.

I made my rounds warily, watching for Sturges, but I soon learned that he'd returned to the drover camp. I half-expected trouble from his boys, but it seemed that trouncing their boss had earned me some grudging respect. The Keogh men made way for me at once wherever I went; there were just a few minor ruckuses that I squelched quietly. Yet it wasn't till the last saloon, the last gambling hall, had closed doors in the gray dawn that I could afford to roll exhaustedly into my blankets.

Next day it was nearly high noon before I roused out, thinking that that sore-lame bear had nothing on me. Shaving and washing up eased away some of the soreness. Then I headed for the cafe for a bite to eat and a word with Bonabeth, if she was speaking. She had an apology due her, and being braced to offer it, I was disappointed to find the Chinaman holding down the place alone. Missy maybe gone to meeting, maybe feeling poorly; not come in, was all he had to offer when I asked where Bonabeth was.

I was finishing up a good meal when Liam Keogh entered and plunked himself on the stool by me, landing a friendly slap between my shoulders that almost unseated me. "Just come from a prayer meetin'," he explained. "Promised my old lady I'd go. Well, lad, old Arch himself couldn't of braced my bunch of curly wolves better'n you did. Handily done!"

I ruefully rubbed my back. "Thank you, sir. Caught an earful about that, did you?"

"Surely did, heh heh, mostly cussing. I'd a give a good saddle, by God, to a seen the Donnybrook with you and that sandy-crawed trail boss o' mine. Got to tell you, though, that ain't done with by a long lick."

"I didn't hazard it was."

"Heh, well, Ralph is been over at the Drovers Saloon this morning—opened it up hisself—busting his belly about how, 'fore he leaves Caprock, he is going to nail up the Hartley hide for fetching flies. Just a word to the wise, son."

"Sure."

Keogh scratched his gray-stubbled chin. "Hartley, I like the cut o' your liver. Takes a man to put Ralph in the dust. But you have put yourself square on a jackpot. He is hell-fire with a hogleg, you know."

"I heard."

"Yeh, well, I tried talking some o' the bile out of his britches, but no luck. You watch your backside, hear? Chinaman, I want the biggest steak in the house, a half-dozen cackle fruit—white wings, mind you, and make 'em flap up 'n' down—and a gallon o' that watered down lye you call coffee. . . ."

Leaving the cafe, I felt a little hollow-bellied for a well-fed man. Whatever happened, though, I still had duties to perform. One was the routine chore of checking the gaming tables in the casinos. I'd once accompanied Arch Benteen on such a round and he'd told me what to look for. Now, a week after his death, there might be some backsliders in the works.

I quartered across to the Nugget, the biggest of Kyle Garth's three gambling houses, and entered. The lofty, garishly furnished room was deserted except for a houseman laying out solitaire at a back table. I gave him a nod and moved over to the roulette wheels. After examining the first one, I straightened up, giving the houseman a swift look. He was watching me warily, hands motionless on his cards. I inspected each wheel in turn, then walked over to him.

"Whereabouts is Garth?"

"His office in back, last I seen."

"Well, suppose you fetch him out here, mister."

The houseman vanished through a rear door. A half a minute later Garth came out, his face bland as butter. "Morning, Marshal."

"Those wheels, Mr. Garth. You're aware they have got crooked attachments rigged on 'em."

He pulled a cigar from a pocket of his brocaded vest, clipped it, and lighted up before answering. "That's right, Hartley."

"For how long?"

"Since a week ago today. Hope you're not too surprised."

"Surprised ain't the word. How green did you reckon I am?"

"Oh, I never doubted your competence, Marshal. I thought we might reach an understanding."

"You want to make that clear?"

Garth smiled crookedly. "You'll recall I suggested that we talk. About this, to be specific. You're a reasonable fellow, aren't you? You always struck me that way."

"Did I?"

"Come on, man. Hadn't you guessed why I argued for you as the new city marshal?"

I stared at him, then said slowly, "Funny, but I didn't. Arch Benteen kept a tight rein on your places. What made you think I wouldn't?"

"Why," Garth said easily, "that's no secret to anyone who knows your prime passion. And everyone in Caprock does."

"You better tell me then."

His smile faded; his eyes narrowed. "Money, Hartley. Christ, you weren't born yesterday, were you?"

His face sort of froze then, I expect from the look on mine.

"Mr. Garth, there's only one understanding you and me require—which is, if them wheels ain't cleaned up before you open tonight, every damn place you control in this town is going to get closed down. Casinos, saloons, everything."

Garth's cigar hit the floor in a shower of sparks. "I've waited a long time to get those attachments in," he said softly. "Why hell, they'd double my . . . look, Hartley, don't be——"

I turned my back on him and walked out.

I'd brooded myself to a low boil by the time I finished my rounds an hour later and returned to the office. Inside, I found Titus Davies standing by the front window and scowling out at the street. His scowl didn't relax as he glanced at me.

"Afternoon, world-beater. Just dropped by to see how —" He broke off, eying me. "What's got you so bug-eyed cheerful?"

I told him. Mr. Davies set his tongue in cheek and said, "Well, well," apropos of nothing.

I stared at him bitterly. "It don't surprise you neither, huh?"

"Simmer down, Sam. *I* backed you at the council meeting for your sterling qualities, remember?"

"But Garth——"

"Done it because he equates money-getting with his own damn crooked style. Reckon you got things to learn about people."

I dropped into my desk chair. "I sure as hell have," I muttered. "The ones in Caprock anyway. That's how you all see me, huh? As a money-grubbing bastard who will do anything—"

"Why," Mr. Davies said mildly, "I never allowed you was a bastard who'll do anything. Nobody but Garth does, that I know of."

"Thanks, thanks all to hell. You make the point damn clear." I shot him a frowning look. "Bonabeth—is that what she thinks? Is that why—"

I checked myself, feeling the blood crawl into my face. Mr. Davies said nothing, just watched me, and finally I said, tight-voiced, "I got reasons for wanting money. It ain't as simple as you all seem to think."

Mr. Davies nodded dryly. "Fine, Sam. Right now, though, I want to tell you about something of interest I seen a few minutes ago, just standing here looking out."

"What's that?"

"Well, that houseman of Garth's, Eb Landers, come out of the Nugget and crossed over to the Drovers' Saloon. Directly he come out with no other than Ralph Sturges, and the two of 'em went back to the Nugget. What's that sound like to you?"

"Like Garth sent Eb to fetch Sturges," I said slowly.

"Yeah. Mighty interesting in the light of what you just said about turning down Garth's bribe. If Kyle can't buy you, might be he thinks he can buy Sturges."

I frowned at him. "For what?"

"Dust off your brains, boy. Ralph is been bragging how he's gonna turn you inside out. Word is got around by now about that. Ralph might just be making drunk talk, but it wouldn't take much to push him to the act. Maybe a good-sized hunk of money changing hands 'ud do it."

"Mr. Davies, that's as good as hiring someone to kill me. Would Garth go that far?"

He made a disgusted sound with his teeth and tongue. "Tried to buy you, didn't he? That's his style; he buys things done. And I don't know any prime topic Kyle and Ralph have got in common outside o' Sam Hartley . . . wait. Look."

Mr. Davies was staring intently out the window again, and I quickly joined him.

A man had just come out of the Nugget Casino down the street, and you couldn't mistake that swagger.

Sturges. He tramped slowly this way, his shoulders pulled high and tense.

"*Marshall!*" he bawled, his voice carrying faintly to us.

"Looks like the moment of truth, Sam," Mr. Davies said quietly.

"Yes, sir. Well, if Sturges has taken Garth's money, he has taken our quarrel outside a private affair. That lets me handle this in an official capacity, don't it?"

"*Marshall!*"

Kyle Garth stepped out of the casino now and stood on its porch, just watching. Sturges was halfway to my office, but walking mighty slow.

I got a box of shotgun shells from the desk, went to the gun rack and took down the long-barreled Greener shotgun. I broke it, slipped in two brass-cased shells and snapped the breech shut. Then I opened the door and stepped outside. Mr. Davies was right behind me; he took a position against the building wall.

I moved out into the high blaze of the sunlit street, holding the shotgun in both hands, pointed down. I could see Sturges' face plain enough, red with heat and whiskey and a rise of baffled rage.

He came to a dead stop, saying thickly, "What the hell is this?"

I judged my range and halted, at the same time leveling the shotgun at him. I did not count on booze slowing him, thinking, he will surely sober fast enough now. "Mr. Sturges, maybe you can pull off a shot at the same time. Maybe you can even break my aim, but from here this gun has enough scatter to get you before I go down. You want to try it?"

A dog barked distantly; a windy plume of dust skittered along the deserted street. Sturges, not moving, swore with a low, savage hoarseness, cussing me till he was even hoarser. It wasn't going to happen, I knew then, at least not this way.

"What I think you should do," I said, "is clear out of Caprock, mister." A dash of theatrics wouldn't hurt; I added, "Before the hour's out, hear?"

I turned on my heel and started back toward the office. My mouth was dry, my nerves wound tight as springs; I had to force a slow easy walk. I finished a step as Mr. Davies yelled, "*Sam, watch it!*"

Without a pause, I fell sideways, diving for the ground as Sturges fired. I was already twisting around on my hip as his second shot kicked up dust a yard away. Hauling the Greener about in a tight arc, hardly taking time to aim, I pulled both triggers.

The double charge roared down the echoes of Sturges' last shot. The lank trail boss was flung backward as if broken in two, his body hitting the dirt with a jolting looseness.

For a long moment I couldn't move. Then, easing the warm stock of the shotgun off my cheek and shoulder, I climbed to my feet. Mr. Davies was beside me, grabbing my arm. "My God, boy, if I hadn't sung out! . . ."

It was a few seconds before I could trust myself to say anything. "I was counting on you to sing out, sir."

Mr. Davies swore feelingly. "You took one hell of a long chance!"

Kyle Garth was heading for the fallen man at a fast walk, and we lost no time getting there ourselves. Garth was already bending over the body when the sound of my Walker Colt being cocked made him jerk upright.

"Stand away from him," I said. "Mr. Davies, will you go through Mr. Sturges' pockets?"

Right away Mr. Davies' search of Sturges' clothes turned up a thin packet of greenbacks. He thumbed quickly through the bills. "Five hunderd dollars—more than this poor shorthorn ever had in his pocket at a time. But a damn small price for what it might help you net, hey, Kyle?"

Sweat beaded Garth's bony face. "You'll have a time proving that money's mine."

"We won't need to," I said. "When this story gets out, no merchant in this town will trade with you. And you won't fetch in customers for sour apples. You're washed up in Caprock, Mr. Garth."

"I'd say so," said Mr. Davies. "Matter of fact, I wouldn't waste no time selling out, packing up and moving on, I was you. If that rigged-wheel business should leak out, kind of by accident, you know, I don't know as how even our sterling marshal could keep you from getting dispatched on a rail with a nice suit of tar and feathers. Purely a shame how rowdy folks hereabouts get sometimes."

Soon as I could that evening, I paid a call on the Connells. Like most of the merchant families, residential homes still being a rarity in the country, they lived on the second story of one of their business places, the mercantile store. Mr. and Mrs. Connell were pleased to see me and Bonabeth did not seem altogether averse. Pretty soon her parents went to the kitchen and left the parlor to us, she on the sofa, me on a hard chair across the room.

She sat in soft lamplight, face bent over her crochet work, fingers busy with it, making the usual small talk banter. And that wasn't what I'd come for.

"Look here, Bonabeth—"

"Yes?" She wasn't giving me a lick of help.

"What about you and Will? Did he ask you to marry him?"

"Of course," she said, as if I were an idiot to ask. Then she looked straight at me and laughed. "About twenty different times, if you have to know."

"Oh."

"A girl likes to be asked, Sam. It's just a formality, but——"

"Look!" My words came in a rush now. "Will has got prospects. If the Lord wanted every man to be a fighter, he'd of made him one. Will is a mighty nice fellow and he has got prospects," I finished lamely.

"Mercy, Sam, you sound like John Alden. That wasn't what you *started* to say, was it?"

"What I started to say was Will has got all his prospects cinched and I am still making mine. That's why I've not been what you can call a proper suitor. I mean, I never thought money was all, but there's things a man wants. . . ."

"Sam." Her smile was gentle. "I know what you want and why. You've told me often enough."

"I guess I have."

"And that might influence a girl's decision to the extent she wants a man to care for her properly. But money isn't the most of all that, and social position is even less. And no woman, whatever she wants for herself and her man, wants to settle for being—well, an accessory to all the rest of it."

I nodded glumly. "Reckon it came out that way, all right, even if I never meant it to."

"Well, what *I* think is, the situation will bear more discussion." She patted the sofa beside her. "And it might be easier for you to talk over here, mightn't it?"

I wasn't sure. But it was.

THE STRANGE VALLEY

The three horsemen came up on the brow of a hill, and the valley was below them. It was a broad cup filled by the brooding thickness of the prairie night. What light was shed by a narrow sickle of moon picked out just another Dakota valley, about a mile across as the white men reckoned distance, and surrounded by a rim of treeless hills. The valley floor appeared to be covered by an ordinary growth of a few small oaks, a lot of brush, and some sandy flats with a sparse lacing of buffalo grass.

Young Elk said, "Is this what you wish us to see, Blue Goose?" He didn't bother to keep the skepticism from his voice.

"Yes," said the rider on his left. "This is the place."

"Now that we're here, tell us again what you saw the other night." The third youth, the shaman's son, sounded very intent. "From where did it come?"

"From there." Blue Goose leaned forward as he pointed toward the eastern end of the valley. "As I told you, I'd had a long day of hunting, and I was very tired. I made my camp in the center of the valley, and fell sleep at once. This was about sunset.

"It was long after dark when I woke. I came awake all

at once, and I don't know why. I heard a strange sound, a kind of growl that was very low and steady, and it was a long way off. But it was running very fast this way, and I sat in my blanket and waited."

Young Elk said with a grim smile, "Because you were too afraid even to run."

Blue Goose was silent for a moment. "Yes," he said honestly. "I was afraid. I didn't know what the thing was, but I knew it was prowling closer. And growling louder all the while, as if in great pain or anger. Then I saw it.

"It was a huge beast, as big as a small hill, black in the night and running very close to the ground, and its two eyes were yellow and glaring. It went past me very close, but so fast I didn't think it saw me. It was bellowing as loud as a hundred bull buffaloes if they all bellowed at once. Suddenly it was gone."

"What do you mean, it was gone?" Young Elk demanded. "You said that before."

"I'm not sure. All I know is that suddenly I saw it no more and heard it no more."

"I wish you could tell us more about it," said the shaman's son. "But I suppose it was very dark."

"Yes," Blue Goose agreed. "Even a little darker than tonight." He hesitated. "I thought that the thing might be covered with scales—bright scales like a huge fish—since the moon seemed to glint on it here and there. But I couldn't be sure."

"You're not very sure of anything," Young Elk gibed.

Blue Goose sighed. "I do not know what I saw. As I have said, I left the valley very fast and camped a long way off that night. But I came back in the morning. I looked for the thing's spoor. I looked all over, and there was nothing. Yet I found where I had camped, and my pony's tracks and my own. But the thing left no sign at all."

"Because there had never been a thing. You should be more careful about what you eat, my friend." Young Elk spoke very soberly, though he felt like laughing out loud. "Spoiled meat in one's belly is like *mui waken*, the strong drink. It has a bad effect on the head."

For a little while the three young Sioux sat their ponies in silence, looking down into the dark stillness of the valley. A silky wind pressed up from the valley floor, a wind warm with the summer night and full of the ripening smells of late summer.

But something in it held a faint touching chill, and that was strange. Young Elk felt a crawl of gooseflesh on his bare shoulders, and he thought, *The night is turning cold, that is all.* He felt the nervous tremor run through his mount.

He laid his hand on the pony's shoulder and spoke quietly to the animal, angry at Blue Goose who was his best friend for telling this foolish story and angry at himself for coming along tonight with the other two because, though skeptical, he was deeply curious. But back in their camp only a few miles to the north there was firelight and laughter and there was a warm-eyed girl named Morning Teal, and Young Elk was a fool to be out here with his friend and with the son of that tired old faker of a medicine man.

Of late, Young Elk thought sourly, there had been more than the usual quota of wild stories of visions and bad spirits running rampant among the people. Early this same summer, on the river of the Greasy Grass that the whites called Little Big Horn, the long-haired general called Custer had gone down to defeat and death with his troops. Many warriors of their own band had been among the twelve thousand Sioux and Cheyenne and Arapaho who had helped in the annihilation of a hated enemy.

In the uneasy weeks since, as the people followed the buffalo, hunting and drying meat in prospect of being soon driven back to the reservation by the white cavalry, a rash of weird happenings had been told. Men who had died were seen walking the prairie with bloody arrows protruding from them. Some claimed to hear the voices of the dead in the night wind. It was the shaman's part to encourage this sort of nonsense. A man claimed that a bluecoat soldier he had scalped appeared to him nightly with the blood still fresh on his head. The shaman had chanted gibberish and told him to bury the scalp so that the ghost would trouble his nights no more.

Young Elk was disgusted. He had never seen even one of these many spirits. Only the fools who believed in such things ever saw them.

The shaman's son broke the long pause, speaking quietly. "This valley is a strange place. Today I spoke with my father and told him what Blue Goose has told us. He said that he knows of this place and that his father's fathers knew of it too. Many strange things happened here in the old days. Men known to be long dead would be seen walking—not as spirits, but in the flesh. Still other things were seen, things too strange to be spoken of. Finally all our people of the Lakotas came to shun the valley. But that was so long ago that most of the old ones, even, have forgotten the old stories."

Young Elk made a rude chuckling sound with his tongue and teeth.

"Young Elk does not believe in such things," the shaman's son observed. "Why then did he come with us tonight?"

"Because otherwise for the next moon I would hear nothing from you and Blue Goose but mad stories about what you saw tonight. I'd prefer to see it for myself."

"Oh," said Blue Goose, "then there *was* something? I did not make this great story out of the air?"

"*Ho-he*," Young Elk said slyly. "Maybe not. Maybe it was the white man's iron horse that Blue Goose saw."

"Now you jest with me. I'm not all-wise like Young Elk, but even I know that the iron horse of the *wasicun* runs on two shining rails, and there are no rails here. And the iron horse does not growl thus, nor does it have two eyes that flame in the dark."

Another silence stretched between the three youths as they sat their ponies on the crest of the hill and peered down into the dark valley. And Young Elk thought angrily, *What is this?* They had come here to go down in the valley and wait in the night in hopes that the thing Blue Goose had seen would make a new appearance. Yet they all continued to sit here as though a winter of the spirit had descended and frozen them to the spot.

Young Elk gave a rough laugh. "Come on!" He kneed his pony forward, putting him down the long grassy dip of hill. The others followed.

Near the bottom, Young Elk's pony turned suddenly skittish; he had to fight the shying animal to bring him under control. Blue Goose and the shaman's son were having trouble with their mounts too.

"This is a bad omen," panted the shaman's son. "Maybe we had better go back."

"No," Young Elk said angrily, for his pony's behavior

and the strange feeling of the place were putting an edge on his temper. "We've come this far, and now we'll see what there is to see, if anything. Where was Blue Goose when he thought he saw the beast?"

Blue Goose said, "We must go this way," and forced his horse through a heavy tangle of chokecherry brush. He led the way very quickly, as though afraid that his nerve would not hold much longer.

They came to a rather open stretch of sand flats that caught a pale glimmer of moonglow. It was studded with clumps of thicket and a few scrub oaks.

"Here is the place," Blue Goose told them.

The three Sioux settled down to wait. Nobody suggested that it would be more comfortable to dismount. Somehow it seemed better to remain on their ponies and accept a cramp or two. It was only, Young Elk told himself, that they should be ready for anything, and they might have a sudden need of the ponies.

Once more it was the shaman's son who ended a speechless interval. "What time of the night did it happen, Blue Goose?"

"I can't be sure. But close to this time, I think."

Silence again.

The ponies shuffled nervously. The wind hushed through some dead brush, which rattled like dry, hollow bird bones. Idly Young Elk slipped his throwing ax from his belt and toyed with it, sliding his hand over the familiar shape of the flint head and the fresh thongs of green rawhide that lashed it to the new handle he had put on only this morning. His palm felt moist and he was slightly dizzy.

The shapes of rocks, the black masses of brush, seemed to shimmer and swim; the landscape seemed misty and unreal as if seen through a veil of fog, yet there was no fog.

It is a trick of the moon, Young Elk thought. He gripped the ax tighter; his knuckles began to ache.

"There!" Blue Goose whispered. "Do you hear it?"

Young Elk snapped, "I hear the wind," but even as the words formed on his lips the sound was increasing, and it was unmistakably *not* the wind. Not even a gale wind roaring through the treetops of a great forest made such a noise. As yet he could see nothing, but he knew that the sound was moving in this direction.

Suddenly the two yellow eyes of which Blue Goose had spoken came boring out of the night.

Young Elk could see the hulking black shape of the monster; it was running toward them at an incredible speed, so low to the ground that they could not see its legs. All the while the weird humming roar it made was steadily increasing.

The ponies were plunging and rearing with fear. The shaman's son gave a cry of pure panic and achieved enough control over his mount to kick it into a run. In a moment Blue Goose bolted after him.

Young Elk fought his terrified pony down and held the trembling animal steady, his own fear swallowed in an eagerness to have a closer look at the thing. But he was not prepared for the fury of its rush as it bore down on him. Its round glaring eyes blinded him—he could see nothing beyond them.

It let out a piercing, horrible shriek as it neared him— it was hardly the length of three ponies away—and it seemed to hesitate. It hissed at him, a long gushing hiss, as the yellow eyes bathed him in their wicked glare.

Young Elk waited no longer. He lunged his pony in

an angling run that carried him past the beast's blunt black snout, and in that moment brought his arm back and flung the ax with all his strength. He heard but did not see it hit with a strange hollow boom, and then he was racing on through the brush, straining low to his pony's withers, heedless of the tearing branches.

Young Elk did not slow till he reached the end of the valley; then he looked back without stopping. There was no sign of the beast. The valley was deserted and quiet under the dim moonlight.

Young Elk crossed the rim of hills and caught up with his friends on the prairie beyond.

"Did you see it?" the shaman's son demanded eagerly.

"No. Its eyes blinded me. But I hit it with my ax." Young Elk paused; his heart was pounding so fiercely in his chest he was afraid they would hear it, so he went quickly on, "I heard the ax hit the thing. So it was not a ghost."

"How do you know?" countered the shaman's son. "Where did it go? Did you see?"

"No," Young Elk said bitterly. "But it was very fast."

"Let's go back to camp," Blue Goose said. "I don't care what the thing was. I do not want to think about it."

Joe Kercheval had been dozing in his seat when his partner, Johnny Antelope, hit the brakes of the big semi-trailer and gave Joe a bad jolt. And then Joe nearly blew his stack when Johnny told him the reason he had slammed to an abrupt stop on this long, lonely highway in the middle of nowhere.

"I tell you, I saw him," Johnny insisted as he started up again and drove on. "A real old-time Sioux buck on a spotted pony. He was sitting his nag right in the middle of the road, and I almost didn't stop in time. Then he came charging past the cab, and I saw him fling something—I think it was an ax—at the truck. I heard it hit. You were waking up just then—you must have heard it."

"I heard a rock thrown up by the wheels hit somewheres against the trailer, that's all," Joe said flatly. "You been on the road too long, kid. You ought to lay off a few weeks, spend a little time with your relatives on the reservation."

Johnny Antelope shook his head. "I saw him, Joe. And then I didn't see him. I mean—I could swear he disappeared—simply vanished into thin air—just as he rode past the cab. Of course it was pretty dark. . . ."

"Come off it. For a college-educated Indian, you get some pretty far-out notions. I've made this run a hundred times and I never seen any wild redskins with axes, spooks or for real."

"You white men don't know it all, Joe. You're Johnny-come-latelies. This has been our country for a long, long time, and I could tell you some things."

Johnny paused, squinting through the windshield at the racing ribbon of highway unfolding in the tunneling brightness of the headlights. "I was just remembering. This is a stretch of land the Sioux have always shunned. There are all kinds of legends concerning it. I remember one story in particular my old granddaddy used to tell us kids. I guess he told it a hundred times or more—"

"Nuts to your granddaddy."

Johnny Antelope smiled. "Maybe you're right, at that. Old Blue Goose always did have quite an imagination."

"So does his grandson." Joe Kercheval cracked his

knuckles. "There's a turnoff just up ahead, kid. Swing around there."

"What for, Joe?"

"We're going back to where you seen that wild man on a horse. I'm gonna prove to you all you seen was moonshine." Joe paused wryly, then added, "Seems like I got to prove it to myself, too. I say it was just a rock that hit the truck, and I'll be losin' sleep if I don't find out for sure."

Without another word Johnny swung the big semi around and headed back east on the highway. The two truckers were silent until Johnny slowed and brought the truck to a shrieking stop. The air brakes were still hissing as he leaned from the window, pointing.

"Here's the spot, Joe. I recognize that twisted oak on the right."

"Okay, let's have a close look."

They climbed out of the cab, and Johnny pointed out the exact spot where he had first seen the Indian warrior, and where the warrior had cut off the highway alongside the cab and thrown his ax.

"Look here, kid." Joe played his flashlight beam over the roadside. "Soft shoulders. If your boy left the concrete right here, his horse would of tromped some deep prints in the ground. Not a sign, see?"

"Wait a minute," Johnny Antelope said. "Flash that torch over here, Joe." He stooped and picked up something from the sandy shoulder.

The halo of light touched the thing Johnny held in his outstretched hand. "Know what this is, Joe?" he asked softly. "A Sioux throwing ax."

Joe swallowed. He started to snort, "Nuts. So it's an ax," but the words died on his lips.

For under the flashlight beam, even as the two men watched, the wood handle of the ax was dissolving into rotted punk, and the leather fastenings were turning cracked and brittle, crumbling away.

Only the stone blade remained in Johnny's hand, as old and flinty and weathered as if it had lain there by the road for an untold number of years. . . .

THE RECKONING

Sundog was aptly named. To say it hadn't changed in five years, Hatch thought, would be like gilding the lily. To him the town had always resembled a tired, slat-ribbed cur dozing in the sun. Clattering to life overnight as a flash in the pan mining town, it had survived as a ranch supply center. But its rows of false-fronted buildings, silvered and scoured by wind and rain and sun, showed its hasty origin.

Hatch reined in his gaunt sorrel by the livery barn. He stepped stiffly out of his saddle, trying to square his bull shoulders in the ill-fitting coat. The suit he wore was good black broadcloth, but sizes too small for his bulk, and grayed by July dust that sifted in streamers from its creases as he tramped into the barn runway, leading the sorrel.

The place was cool and dim, smelling of musty straw and the sharp ammoniac reek of dung. An unconscious scowl knit Hatch's thick black brows as he halted in the clay-floored runway, blinking against the red ache of his eyes. This old barn hadn't changed either, except for being more run-down than ever.

Christ. What a place for a kid to grow up.

For a moment the tingle of anticipation Hatch felt was

beat down by an unaccustomed twitch of panic. What did you say to a kid after five years? Tell had been only thirteen when he'd gone away. There'd been a few letters from the boy over the first couple years. After that, nothing at all.

Jesus, five years. Time enough for a boy to shape toward manhood, to change.

"Anybody here?" His voice carried hollow between the double row of stalls; a horse whickered irritably.

Moon Forney came out of the office at the rear of the barn, an immensely fat man who swayed as he stumped down the runway. A single gallus supported the greasy leather pants he wore over dirty underwear. His bloodshot eyes squinted above an ambush of tangled gray whiskers.

He came to a stop, his jaw dropping.

"I be damn . . . Hatch. Lucas Hatch. It really you?"

"Me all right." Hatch stuck out his hand, noting that Moon's was damp with sudden sweat as he gripped it. "Still batting the jug, eh?"

Moon gave a nervous titter. "It shows, huh?"

What the hell, thought Hatch. He's scared.

"Where is he, Moon?"

Moon fingered his beard, grinning vaguely. "Didn't have no idea you was getting out, Lucas. You oughta get a man word."

Hatch's hand, scarred and hamlike, shot out and seized a handful of underwear, then hauled the liveryman forward till their faces were inches apart.

"You act kind of skittery, Moon. Why is that?"

"Jeezus, Lucas! You don't need to take aholt of a man like—"

Hatch's fist twisted, forcing Moon's sagging bulk up on

its toes. "Then you give a man a straight answer when he asks you. *Where's my boy, Moon?*"

"He's all right! Tell's all right! God's sake, Lucas, you choking me!"

Hatch slowly unclenched his hand. "It could get worse, old man. A whole sight worse. Where's Tell?"

Moon backed off a step; his wreath of chins shook. "Now you listen, old Moon done his best, Lucas. He done his level best, you hear?"

"Moon, I ain't going to ask you again."

"He gone to work for Santee Quillan, Tell has. It wa'n't no doing of mine, Lucas."

Hatch felt a deep sinking in his belly. He didn't move, just stared at Moon, who took another step back.

"Don't be skittery," Hatch said softly. "No reason to be, less'n it's your blame."

"Lucas, I swear t' you——"

"Let's step back to your office, all right?"

Moon led the way into the dirty cubbyhole. He lifted a jug from under his battered roll-top desk, yanked the cork, and took a big slug. Hatch, his stare like jagged slate, grabbed the jug away and slammed it down on the desk.

"Don't stall me, Moon. Just don't stall me."

"All right—all right! It happent like this. . . ."

He hadn't been able to control the boy, Moon insisted. Young Tellford had taken to hanging out with a pool hall crowd, riding high with the young toughs on the strength of his father's reputation. About a year ago some county ranchers had started complaining of penny ante rustling; talk was that Tell and his crowd of young hoodlums were mixed in it. Sheriff Buckhart had figured he had enough evidence to jail the lot.

But before trial, the sheriff had been shot in the back from an alley. The killer was never found. Grudge murder, was the verdict of the coroner's inquest, but it was whispered that Santee Quillan was behind that killing of an honest lawman; he'd done it in order to cinch his growing power in the county. A gun-handy henchman of Santee's, Gauche Sevier by name, had been appointed by Santee's friend, Judge Harkness, to take over the sheriff's office. Tellford Hatch and his friends had never come to trial; Santee had put up their bail money and then the case was quietly dropped. These days Tell was seen everywhere with Santee's hardcase bunch.

Hatch took off his hat and swiped a hand over his face, slowly rubbing his eyelids.

Lord God. Where had it all started?

Ten years ago he'd been a respected rancher with a wife and a sturdy young son and a home full of love and laughter—enough to do any man proud. Then he had suffered one stinking setback after another—tearing all of his work down, tearing him down as a man. First there had been the typhoid plague and Lena's death, then the drought that had turned his summer graze tinder-dry, and the prairie fire that had wiped out his grass and buildings. Finally there had been the desperate trail drive to Dodge to salvage something, anything. A sudden attack of Texas fever had left his herd strung out dead and dying along the banks of the Red River.

Back in his home country he'd organized several equally desperate neighbors for rustling strikes against still-thriving outfits, running the stolen beeves on night drives down to the Gulf Coast and a rendezvous with crooked stock buyers. In a few years Hatch had gathered a gang of tough nuts and held them together with a hard fist and a quick gun. Lucas Hatch—gunman, rustler, gang leader notorious. Everyone had known it; none had had the proof or the nerve to do anything about it. Hatch's headquarters had been G-Town, a backwoods hellhole frequented by ne'er-do-wells and bad characters of every stripe. He'd left his growing son with Moon Forney in Sundog, paying for the boy's care.

But Hatch and his gang had gone too far when they'd broken into a Union Pacific mail car and carried off ten thousand dollars in government gold. And Hatch had been identified by a trainman. Dick Clendennon, the tough U.S. deputy marshal, had come alone to G-Town and calmly walked into a dive where Hatch and his gang were drunkenly celebrating. Clendennon had hit Hatch over the head with his gun, shot one of the gang who objected, carried Hatch out, slung him over a horse, and taken him to trial and a twenty-year sentence in the penitentiary.

Hatch dropped his hand, feeling the scarred-over pain surge alive once more. *Lena, Lena!* If only she had lived. But that wasn't right either; it was like blaming the dead. He had paved his own road; it was too late for turning back.

But there was still Tell.

Moon Forney was rummaging in his desk; he dug out a pair of tin cups and sloshed both full from the jug and handed one to Hatch. "Uh, you got a parole, huh?"

Hatch looked at the cup a moment, then swigged down a gulp of the raw whiskey, feeling it curl like hellfire in his belly. "Yeah," he said heavily. "Lucas Hatch, model prisoner. Feature that, Moon."

Relieved at being off the hook, Moon gave a jowl-shaking chuckle.

Hatch stared into the cup. "Santee Quillan must of taken some pepper in his craw since we rode together. He always talked a big game, but I never seen him into anything bigger'n two-bit cow-lifting."

Moon swallowed his whiskey to the last drop before replying. "Yeh, yeh, he runs the county now. Got his finger in ever' damn pie that's cut. Year after you was sent away, he busted the Alhambra Casino in a big game, bet his whole pile against the house and won that. Bought a freighting business and hired gunnies to force his rivals to sell out cheap. Now he owns all the saloons in Sundog, the general store, feed company, most everything."

"Is that right?"

"Surest damn thing you know." Moon lowered his voice. "Runs a local rustling combine too. Sells stolen beef through special contacts he's got down in Williamson County. Got 'most ever' elected official hereabouts under his thumb. He ain't stopping there neither. Got him some heavy pull with a political machine up in Austin, they say. . . ."

Hatch nodded slowly.

Santee had always been slick as silk, too slick for any honest crook's taste. But his smooth ways had been helpful in disposing of the crowd's stolen beef to crooked dealers. One time, when he'd tried to skip out with all the proceeds and they'd caught him, the rest had been for hanging him. But Hatch had made an object lesson of Santee instead, beating him to a pulp in front of them all.

It had seemed a good idea at the time, but Santee wasn't the kind to forget; he would hold a grudge forever, biding his time. Knowing Santee's ability to hold a grudge hadn't troubled Hatch's sleep; he'd never been all that impressed by Santee Quillan. But he knew never to turn his back on the man, that was all.

That was one more mistake you made, Hatch thought. It could just have been the biggest of them all.

He drained his cup, hitting Moon with a slate-hard look. "You could of got word to me about Tell."

"Ha-ha, now you know I can't write none, Lucas. Anyways, locked up like you was, nothing you could do, was there?"

"Where'll he be now?"

Moon shrugged. "Kind o' early, but I'd try the Alhambra. Him and that frenchified sheriff of Santee's are thicker'n horseflies in July. Drinkin', gamblin', wenchin' around. . . ."

Hatch didn't say any more. He walked out to the street and swung south through the midday glare toward the Alhambra's garish sign a block away. His hand curled unthinkingly along his thigh, as if to grip a gun that wasn't there.

The hand began to perspire and he wiped it dry on his coat.

Shoving through the batwing doors into a smell of sawdust and stale whiskey, he swung a glance across the mahogany bar and tables. The place was deserted except for a corner table where two men were bent over cards. One threw down his hand with a curse and tilted his chair back, swinging his profile into relief.

Hatch's heart thudded to his steps, hollow on the long floor, as he crossed to the table. Neither man even glanced at him.

He cleared his throat gently.

Tell turned his head. His bored young face went slack

with disbelief. He got up so quickly that his chair crashed to the floor.

"Pa! My God! *You?*"

Hatch had the swift, brief shock of seeing the gangling boy he remembered facing him at eye level. A second shock came with what he saw in the youth's face. They had always looked a lot alike, he and Tell, and now it was as if he faced his own mirror likeness of twenty and more years ago.

But there were differences too. Hatch had worked too hard in his youth to enjoy the kind of fast living that showed in Tell's face. *Christ, he's only eighteen!* Hatch thought wildly.

After a long, awkward moment, he stuck out his hand and Tell took it awkwardly. Another difference. His own palms wore a thick horn of callus from prison work. Tell's were soft.

"You, ah, get paroled, Pa? That it?"

Hatch nodded. He was having trouble finding words.

"Well, Jesus—" Tell's grin steaked wide and sudden across his face. "You *look* good."

"Yeah. Outside work. We got plenty of that."

"Your pa, Tell? This so fine looking man is your pa?"

The other cardplayer had a soft lazy voice, finely accented, and his fingers, gently riffling the cards, were long and fine. He stayed lazily slack in his chair, not offering to shake hands, merely nodding with a chalky little grin as Tell jerkily performed the introductions.

Gauche Sevier. Hatch knew the name but not the man. Sevier had a full, olive-colored face, his long black hair pulled to a sleek club at the back of his neck. A Creole dandy from the Louisiana side of the Sabine, Hatch guessed. Sevier's gun belt was cinched low on his fawn-colored pants; a sheriff's star glinted on his brocaded vest.

"Lucas Hatch," he murmured. It was the purr of a relaxed cougar. "Your prowess with the gun was heard of to New Orleans once. It sets a man to wondering."

"Well," Hatch said, "I hope you ain't too curious."

Sevier laughed, rounding his eyes. "Ah! If one is the better, *n'est ce pas?* But *non!* Against the father of my so great friend Tell? Ah, *non.*"

"You relieve me."

Tell chuckled, a little nervously. "How about a drink, Pa?"

"I want to talk to you."

"Hell, you can say it in front of Gauche."

Hatch rolled his shoulders against the tight coat, feeling the anger in him gather and focus now. Just take it slow, he warned himself. It's been five years since you saw him.

A door opened at the rear of the long room.

"Lucas, by God!" Santee Quillan was coming forward, hand extended. "Thought I knew that voice. How you doing, boy?"

Nothing to do but set your teeth and dog it out, Hatch told himself. Somehow.

Except for the pearl-gray suit tailored to his blocky body, Santee Quillan hadn't changed. His light hair was close-cropped above an oval cherub's face. Even as a nondescript and unshaven cow thief, he'd used that bland boyish charm to pave over every bump in his crooked road. Shaved and bay rummed, he was no different. He could afford men like Gauche Sevier to handle the bumps that wouldn't smooth out, that was all.

After another pleasantry or two, Santee took a couple of cigars from a waistcoat pocket and held one out.

"No," Hatch said. "Thanks."

"Well, well." Santee clipped his cigar with a small gold cutter. "Old Lucas. I can't believe it," he said, smiling the smile that never reached his eyes as he lighted the cigar. "Things have changed, you know, boy. A lot of things."

"I heard."

"Well, well. No point mincing words, then. There's a good place for you in my outfit if you want it—where you can keep an eye on Tellford." He dropped a hand on Tell's shoulder. "Coming up quite a young man, ain't he?"

Hatch held himself in with an effort.

"Like you say," he said tonelessly. "I got something to tell you, Santee. Private."

"I thought you might have. Mind stepping outside, Tell?"

Tell looked uncertain; he glanced from one to the other.

"Do it, son," Hatch said tightly.

"Well, hell, ain't I got a right—"

"You heard your daddy," Santee smiled. "Take a walk, boy."

Tell wheeled and tramped angrily out the batwing doors.

Santee flicked a fractional ash from his cigar. "Don't mind if Gauche here listens in, do you?"

"Like you said, no point mincing words. Santee, I come back to Sundog for one reason—to see my boy set a straight trail. You're fouling it. So step off. Just step off it, Santee."

"Um. So Lucas Hatch seen the light and done reformed. Quite a joke, eh, Gauche?"

Sevier showed his chalky smile. "It is a great joke."

"Don't be dumb, Santee. You don't want to tangle with *state* law. He's still under age and I'm still his father."

Santee's eyes widened mockingly. "Pardon me all to hell. Guess you didn't know the court appointed old Moon Forney Tell's legal guardian after you was sent up."

"I know it and it don't matter. Moon'll follow my lead."

"Lucas, you just don't get it, do you? You made your last tracks five years ago. I hold the whip hand now. Moon knows it. And you know Moon."

Hatch felt a cling of sweat along his belly and back. He made his voice steady. "Santee, I know why you took Tell on. But you won't need him now."

Santee lifted his brows. "No?"

"I'm here. You can do what you want with me. You don't need to stab me through the kid. Let him go."

"Who's holding him? He likes it with me."

"You can get him off that idea."

"I swear, Lucas, you must of spent your time in prison reading bad novels. Can't think where else you'd a picked up all these notions. I made you an offer. Come on. Have a drink, think it over."

Hatch shuttled a glance at Sevier who was on his feet now, standing negligently, a thumb hooked in his gunbelt.

Hatch said calmly, "All right. You're forcing my hand is all. Santee, you was in on that last holdup. I could of turned state's evidence and knocked years off my term by turning in the lot of you."

Santee nodded unconcernedly. "You want me to thank you?"

"After my release, I told the warden to get word to the U.S. deputy marshal to come to Sundog and meet me here. He ought to be along in a day or so."

Santee's eyes narrowed. "Clendennon?"

"Clendennon was never satisfied with just nailing me. I was the only one they could identify for certain. Clendennon wanted all the men in on that holdup. He visited me in prison regularly, tried to pump me, I never broke. Be a different story when he gets here. That—or you shuck Tell off your payroll."

"Lucas, that's a poor bluff. You didn't know what was happening with Tell till just now. I'd swear it."

"You ever hear of a prison grapevine, Santee?"

Santee's tongue flicked over his lips; slowly he shook his head. "No, Lucas. It's a bluff. It won't wash. That time you beat me to a pulp in front of a half a dozen others? No one ever done that to me and I ain't forgot it. Prison put you out of my reach, but not your son. I meant to build him up to worse than the swellhead pup he is, then frame him and throw him to the law." He laughed quietly. "No way I can hurt you like that'll hurt you. Is there, Lucas?"

A red darkness sizzled in Hatch's brain. He saw Santee's pale smiling face, and only that.

He smashed out once, solidly.

Santee backpedaled wildly and crashed into the table, taking it over with him as he fell.

"Don't move, M'sieu." Sevier barely whispered the words. "It is better a man has an even break, eh?"

Hatch rubbed a shaking hand across his mouth. He

looked at the Creole's cocked and leveled pistol and slowly, slowly, let his weight relax on his heels.

Santee got to his feet, fumbling out a silk handkerchief. He dabbed at his cut lip. He wiped his hands, eying Hatch smilingly.

"You're a fool. How about that Sevier, eh? Ever see anyone so fast with a hogleg?"

"He dumb enough to use it?"

"Don't make that mistake. Gauche will drop you in your tracks if I say the word. Of course Tell won't be happy about that, but——" Santee let one shoulder lift and fall. "He won't be unhappy long, I guarantee it. Oh yes, I can cover both your deaths, Lucas. Sundog's my town. I can cover any damn thing that happens in it."

Hatch didn't reply. A sick taste of defeat filled his mouth.

"About Clendennon. That *was* a bluff, eh?"

"Go to hell."

"Lucas, I can cover a deputy marshal's death too, if I have to. You better answer up."

"All right. It was a bluff."

Santee smiled pleasantly. "I believe you. You just saved your hide, boy. Your kid's, too. Tell you what, now. The stage from the north will be here at one. Its run will take you south almost to the border. From there you can spit into Mexico. Get over the river, Lucas. Don't let me hear of you on this side of it again, all right?"

"What about Tell?"

"You can't do him no good. Won't be you he'll listen to after today. Understand?" The smile again. "What we'll do now, we'll all amble down to Moon's and wait for that stage. They switch teams there. You'll want to say so long to Tell. But careful how you say it, Lucas. Careful."

Hatch walked out ahead of the two.

Tell was pacing slowly up and down by the livery barn as they approached it, head down, thumbs hooked in his belt. He hauled up now, dropped his hands. There was no surprise in his young face; it looked guarded and sullen.

"Your pa has got to be on his way," Santee said easily. "Too bad he can't stay a spell. Pressing business, he says, down Mexico way."

Tell didn't seem to hear him. He looked at his father. "You letting 'em hooraw you out, ain't you?"

"Like he says, that's all. You take care yourself, boy."

"I always looked up to you." Tell's voice was soft and bitter and wondering. "Man, I always bragged you up to anyone'd pay ear. Always thought if you come back, man, what a pair we'd make."

"You thought that, did you, boy?"

"Hell!" Tell half-shouted it. "I know there's bad blood 'twixt you and Santee! You think I didn't hear about that? But you lost your nerve. I knew it when you walked into the Alhambra 'thout no gun on! You lost your guts or you wouldn't 'a' come to Sundog without a gun!"

Hatch glanced at Santee drawing unconcernedly on his cigar, then at Sevier who stood idly hip-cocked, one hand resting on his hip, index finger idly tapping the butt of his gun. He gave Hatch the edge of a warning smile.

Even if Santee didn't hold every card, what could he say? He'd given this boy of his nothing to hold pride in but a gunman and outlaw. Now even that warped grain of respect was wiped out.

It wouldn't matter what he said. The twig was bent. And Lucas Hatch—more than Santee Quillan, more than anything—had done the bending.

Santee eyed Tell, slowly nodding. "You're a bright lad, Tellford. Yes, sir. But hell, I knew it from the first. I didn't single you out from that bunch of punks you ran with for nothing."

Tell said nothing. Did he believe Santee? Hatch wondered.

Even so, Hatch thought sickly, you can't let it go like this. There has got to be something you can do for the boy.

Moon Forney came from the archway of the stable, leading the teams of swing horses. He halted, seeing the four of them, and scraped a palm nervously over his whiskered jaw.

"You, uh, leaving here, Lucas? Had kind of a feeling you wouldn't be 'round long. Didn't even unrig your hoss—"

"Lucas has decided to take the stage," Santee said idly. "He won't need a horse. Pay him what it's worth, Moon."

"Not much, that crow bait," mumbled Moon. "Ain't worth more'n twenty dollars."

"He'll take it. Get the money and his saddle." A wicked mockery flicked Santee's tone. "You want your saddle, don't you, Lucas? You can trade it for a barrel of sour wine down in pepper-gut country."

In a couple of minutes Moon came out lugging the saddle and dropped it to the ground. The stage, with a thunder of hooves and rattle of harness, came rolling in from the north end of town as Moon thumbed some bank notes off a greasy wad of them and handed them to Hatch, not meeting his eyes. Hatch pocketed the bills and bent to pick up his saddle.

The stage careened to a stop in front of the archway. Santee moved over to the front boot, saying to the driver, "Any mail this trip, Bowie?"

Hatch tramped toward the rear boot holding his saddle. He glanced through the stage window at its single passenger. Then, facing the coach broadside, he froze in his tracks, a coldness balling his guts.

He saw a hawk face chiseled from brown granite, the hawk eyes fixing him like a target. For a moment he couldn't believe it. And then he didn't want to.

Clendennon.

Santee was still talking to the driver, and Sevier's face was turned that way. Yet Hatch was paralyzed for the moment. Clendennon's arm thrust out the window and turned the door latch. His tall form bent almost double through the tight doorway as he began to step down.

Santee's gaze swung casually toward him.

Shock blazed across Santee's face. Then his hand darted into his coat and came out with a double-barreled pocket pistol.

"Gauche, that's Clendennon!"

Sevier's hand blurred down and up, cocking his gun as it came level.

Clendennon's hard eyes moved from Hatch to Santee. "Quillan, what the hell is this?"

"You'll never know," Santee whispered. His lips pulled back from his teeth. "You bluff better than I knew, Lucas. Now there'll be an incident of sorts. A deputy marshal and a stage driver were killed in Sundog by an unknown gunman. That's all anybody will ever find out. You bluffed too damn well, Lucas. Now you'll watch it the way I said."

Tell stood white and slack-jawed as the Creole's .45 swung to cover him. Lifting Tell's gun from its holster, Sevier dropped it in his coat pocket. He twitched a faint, sorrowful shrug.

"I am sorry for this, my friend. You were a *bon ami*—"

Whirling suddenly, Hatch threw his saddle, thrusting it out with the heels of his hands and releasing his grip.

The heavy rig, backed by all the force of his heavy arms and shoulders, hit Sevier in the chest and knocked the slender gunman spinning, his gun blasting off to one side. He fell over the coach tree and rolled between the wheel horses.

In the same instant Hatch drew in his body and lunged sideways at Santee. The pocket pistol barked almost in his face. Hatch felt a sledging impact in his arm. Then he slammed full tilt into Santee and they went down together.

Santee landed on his back, clawing and kicking against Hatch's weight. His right arm was doubled against his chest, pinned there by Hatch's body. Then he yanked it free, clubbing his pistol blindly at Hatch's head. A savage cuff of Hatch's fist sent the weapon flying. Hatch surged to his feet, dragging Santee with him.

A gunshot crashed behind them, but Hatch didn't turn his head. All the pent-up fury in him boiled out in one smashing blow. Santee's knees folded. Hatch held him erect by a fistful of shirtfront, pulling his other fist back for another full-arm blow.

"That's enough!"

Clendennon's voice cracked like a whip. Hatch swung a red stare at the lawman and his drawn pistol. Then he let Santee's limp body crumple to the ground.

Sevier lay face down in the dirt where he'd scrambled from beneath the team. Blood darkened the dust by his head.

"Had to shoot," Clendennon said. "He was pulling a bead on your back. You hit?"

Hatch grimaced. The numbness was going from his arm and the pain had begun, savage and tearing. Blood dripped off the ends of his fingers. His knees felt weak. He had the deathly feel of a man reaching the end of something.

"Still no sawbones in this town, I take it," said Clendennon.

"No sir," Moon said shakily. "I got some redeye back in the office."

Tell was still rooted where he stood, his face white and stunned.

"You——" Clendennon's voice made Tell jump as if he'd been stung. "Give your pa a hand inside."

Santee Quillan groaned. Clendennon gave Hatch a hard wry look, then pulled a set of handcuffs from his pocket, bent and snapped them on Santee's wrists and hauled him to his feet.

Supported by his son, Hatch tramped down the stable runway to the office. Clendennon growled an order that held back a handful of people drawn by the ruckus, then followed with Santee in tow. Hatch settled himself on the single rickety chair in Moon's office. After he'd taken a slug of whiskey, Clendennon helped him work off his coat.

"You give this garment quite a stretch," the lawman observed dryly. "That drummer's just middling size."

Hatch eyed him dully. "Thought here'd be the last place the law would think I'd come. And how in hell you catch up so fast? I come straight here after busting out."

"Don't be a damn fool," Clendennon grunted. "Where else would Lucas Hatch go?"

He talked tersely as he cut away the bloody shirt from Hatch's arm with his pocket knife. He said that the warden had telegraphed his office, informing him that Hatch had escaped from a gang working outside the walls. Clendennon, judging Hatch would head nowhere but where his son was, had picked up the trail at once. His horse had gone lame on the road, the lawman said, or he'd have made better time. Walking into the swing station fifty miles north of here, Clendennon had spoken with a traveling man who'd been attacked on the road by a fellow in convict's clothes, a man who'd come barreling out of the brush, leaped on the drummer's wagon and knocked him out. When the drummer had come to, his clothes were gone and one of the horses, as well as a saddle rig from his sales stock.

"Somehow," Clendennon concluded in his dry, acid way, "I concluded I was on the right track."

Moon Forney's jaw dropped. "I be dogged. They wa'n't no parole, huh? He busted out——"

"I'm wondering why," Clendennon said grimly. "He had a fine prison record. Would of got half his sentence knocked off for good behavior. He knew damn well I'd track him into Mexico if I had to."

Hatch stirred his shoulders wearily. "Even another

year in the pen was too long, way I felt. I had no word from my boy. I had to see him once more—see how he was."

Tell was leaning his back to the wall, arms folded, staring doggedly at the floor. He didn't look up. But he moved in a hurry when Clendennon, after examining the wound, snapped at him to lend a hand.

The bullet had passed clean through without touching bone and the exit wound wasn't as bad as Hatch had feared. That lady's gun of Santee's, Clendennon observed as he cleaned and bandaged the hurt, wasn't worth shucks past a yard away.

Finished, Clendennon jerked a curt nod at Santee sitting on the floor, cuffed hands wiping his bleeding nose with a handkerchief.

"I want to hear what happened with him. All of it."

Hatch told him, watching Tell as he talked. Before he was done, the boy was looking straight at him.

"I—I should of known better." Tell swallowed hard. "You was letting Santee run you out to keep us both alive. I thought—well, I thought you'd changed—"

"He changed," Clendennon said in a flat cold voice. "Cut sign on this, boy. Kind of bargain-sale guts it takes to make Santee's kind of crook ain't worth a penny on the dollar. I kept a close track on your pa in prison. It never changed him. I never seen prison make a better man of anyone. Hatch changed himself. If you don't know yet why he done it, well boy, you just wasn't worth it."

Tell flushed. "Guess I see it all right."

"I reckon so will the governor. He happens to be a friend of mine." Clendennon rubbed his chin, jutting it in the way of a man who'd made up his mind. "We're that close, we don't balance out favors no more. All the same, I don't ask 'em lightly. I got to know a man. I got to know your pa pretty well, hoorawing him off and on these five years. Might of stepped in for him before except he never would give me some names I wanted."

Tell's mouth opened. "You mean Pa—you can fetch Pa a pardon?"

"Not right off, no. Not after he busted prison. But there's his reason and some good results besides. Santee here, we been trying to get some goods on him a long time. That's enough to get things moving." Clendennon's cold glance shifted to Hatch. "He's got a lot going for him, your pa. The governor's a family man. Knows what it is to have a son get steered the right way."

Hatch felt shaky with more than pain. He started to his feet, then winced and sank back. "Lend me a hand, Tell——"

It was good to see his son move as fast to that quiet order as he had to Clendennon's tough ones.

POINT OF HONOR

Kjerstin saw the rider when he was still a long way down the valley.

She was scattering feed to the chickens, pausing to pick up her small pet hen and stroke it, the only bird in the flock that didn't resent such attentions, crooning to it in Swedish—"*Var en snall, min flicka*"—when she glanced across the flats to the north and saw the horseman come down through the Notch.

For a moment Kjerstin watched him, shading her eyes against the late afternoon sun. Unhurriedly now, she set the hen down, shook the rest of the feed out of her pan, then turned and walked back to the house. She moved easily and with only a hint of tiredness, though a long day's work lay behind her. At twenty-five she was lithe and strong, and bore the three months of her pregnancy lightly. Hard work and hard living she could bear with a will, better than the leaden kernel of worry that lived in her stomach, as real and constant as the growing child in her womb.

Maybe the rider was Anders coming home, but at this distance Kjerstin could not tell. As always, she would take no chance.

The kernel of worry grew heavier whenever her husband was gone, and he had been gone since the day before yesterday. Anders was a jack-of-all-trades; he had been everything from a schoolteacher to a trail boss while still in his twenties, and he was a skilled doctor of animals, second to none in the county. That was why Mr. Blivens, who owned a big ranch over west, had sent a cowhand to fetch Anders to treat some colic-afflicted cows. When he went on such an errand, there was no saying when he would be back. She never complained, but Anders was sensitive to her feelings. She remembered his words just before he had left: "Be patient, *käresta*. John Blivens pays money for work, and the money we need. It will not always be this way. A year or two of good crops will make the difference, and then I will not need to hire out to others. . . ."

Kjerstin hoped that time was not far off. Until then, however, she kept the big shotgun close by the door whenever Anders was gone. He had showed her how to use it; she knew what it would do to anything that threatened her or what was hers.

Stepping into the log house now, she picked the weapon up, a cool and solid reassurance in her hands, and stepped outside to wait, again shading her eyes to watch the coming rider. The wind molded her calico dress against her tall, firm body and toyed with the free strands of her pale hair.

The man was soon close enough for her to be sure he was not Anders—the horse was a big iron-gray, not Anders' rawboned piebald—and the sharpening worry quickened her pulse. She had seen that horse before.

She began to raise the shotgun before Croy Bleeker was two hundred feet away. It was butted firmly against her shoulder, though pointed down enough not to line on him, as he pulled his dancing mount up perhaps six yards away.

Bleeker was a big man, tall and heavy-boned, but whipped to a rawhide spareness, gaunt as a timber wolf in January. The slight stoop to his strong shoulders came more from work and harsh living—those signs she knew well—than from age, though he was about sixty. His face was a brown crag, jut-chinned and hawk-beaked. Weather tracks crowfooted his cheeks and eye corners; a droop of ragged white mustaches hid his jaws and mouth. Bleeker was a lifelong bachelor—a woman-hater it was said—and it showed in his untrimmed hair and old, unmended clothes, as shabby as those of any man who worked his cattle.

He eyed her for a moment out of the shadow of his hat, then said abruptly, "Your man about?"

"No. What is it you want, Mr. Bleeker?"

"Where is he?"

"Gone to John Blivens' to see after the sick cows. I do not know when he comes back. Why do you come here?"

Croy Bleeker leaned forward, fisting both hands on his pommel. "You know damn well why I'm here, missus. I told you people the Box Eighty line goes way south of the Notch. You're inside my line."

"*Ja*, you have told us——"

"I come to tell you for the last damn time. What does it take, by God, to pound something into your thick snorkie heads?"

Kjerstin felt the bitter rise of her blood. "You know this is a homestead and we have made the improvements like the law says. Maybe it is your head too thick to understand good, eh?"

Bleeker studied her a moment, then spat across his arm. "You know what a nester is?"

"*Ja*, it is what you call us who homestead."

"You know why?"

She shook her head watchfully, taking a better grip on the shotgun.

He looked slowly around him, at the small, tight cabin and the outbuildings and the half-built log barn. His look was heavy with contempt. Then he swept an arm at the piles of brush stacked along the edge of the wide clearing. "That's why. You clear back the brush and it looks like a big rat's nest with your goddamn shacks in the middle."

That, Kjerstin thought angrily, was a personal affront; no people prided themselves on tidy habits more than did Swedes. "We not yet got to burning the brush," she said with dignity. "There been so much other things, there is still so much to do—"

"You don't get it, missus," he declared harshly. "This is been open range since I come here twenty years ago. I lived, et, drunk, slept, rode, walked and run on free range all my life. There ain't no other way for a man to live. I can't sleep nights knowing there's a scab like this place inside ten miles of my ranch headquarters."

"So," Kjerstin said coldly, "then do you ride back to it, mister, and next time you bring your men and then you all tell me, eh?"

Saddle leather creaked as he shifted his weight, shaking his head. "I shot my own dogs all my life. There was some Injuns squatting in this same valley when I first clapped eyes on it. I drove them out 'thout no help and I'll clean out you nesters same way."

Bleeker swung to the ground, his movements stiff but

light, and dropped his reins. Deliberately she cocked back both hammers of the shotgun and leveled the weapon on his chest.

He hesitated, chewing his mustache and glaring. Kjerstin awaited his next move, her heart pounding. She felt no doubt at all as to what she would do if necessary. . . .

Only a few short months ago, that thought would have shocked and terrified her. But already the girl she'd been seemed another person from another world. It had become so since the day their heavy-ladened Conestoga had rolled into this valley, the valley that Anders had first seen three years ago and had resolved to settle one day. Springing down from the wagon, he had dug his fingers deep into the grass, into the soil, bringing up a handful to show her its black richness. And Kjerstin had known from the light in his face that her man had come home at last; this was what he wanted most after all his wanderings, his work in many trades, to own and till a piece of land as his fathers had before him in *gamla hemlandet*, the old country. In that moment she'd known against all misgivings that she must share his determination as, on their wedding day, she had vowed to share his life.

At that time Croy Bleeker and his men had been driving a herd to Montana, where the rancher had a contract with an Indian agent to supply his reservation wards with beef. When they'd returned, the Halsteds' clearing had been made and their cabin put up. Shortly after, a Box Eighty rider had spotted it and reported it to his boss. That was three weeks ago, and Croy Bleeker had paid them a first visit and issued a first warning. A week ago he had come again with harsher words and a straight-out threat. Now, quite plainly, he meant business; she could feel the man's rage, the fire in him of a decision made.

She remembered how Anders had bluntly summed up the matter. "We have no choice, *käresta*. I have seen in Nebraska what some cattlemen do to people with homesteads, burning them out, running them off. The law does not help where there is no lawman. This county is hundreds of square miles across, and here we are cut off by mountains." He'd shaken his head regretfully. "I didn't think we would know trouble like this. Maybe it will not come to fighting, maybe Herr Bleeker only makes a bluff. But we must be ready . . . for anything."

Now Herr Bleeker had made his decision. But so had they. She hoped he understood that.

His eyes were stony and unrelenting. "You better put that scattergun down, missus. You ain't going to use it."

"I hope you do not believe this." Kjerstin framed her thought with great care in the English that—less than a year out of her native Sweden—she still handled with difficulty. "I hope I do not have to show you."

Bleeker took a quick step forward.

"*Håll!* I do not tell you again, —" She wrinkled her nose. "*Ugh, du gris!*"

"What's that?"

"You. . . ." She groped for the word. "You stink."

The blood darkened his face. Again he moved, taking two steps, but slowly. For an instant her finger tensed to the trigger.

Then Bleeker's head turned. He said something, softly, that sounded like a curse. He was looking off toward the Notch, the only clear entrance to the valley through the tall hills and thick timber, as if he saw someone.

But Kjerstin did not take her eyes off him; he would not trick her so easily.

Yet as he continued to stare, she felt a nudge of concern. Suppose it was one of his men coming? Very cautiously, not taking her eyes off Bleeker, she turned her head just enough to cover the Notch from the tail of her eye. *Ja*, someone was coming. A rider. Could it be Anders returning? *Let it be Anders!*

The moments seemed to drag eternally as the rider drew nearer. He was very close then, coming up the last rise below the barn, and her heart sank. Not Anders. A stranger who might be one of Bleeker's crew or—

Her attention had strayed, if not her eyes; she watched Bleeker, yet no longer saw him. And sensing it, or only taking a wild chance, he moved like a great cat, swiftly and suddenly, hammering the shotgun aside with a sweep of his hand as Kjerstin jerked both fingers. Her ears still rang with its thunder as he wrenched the weapon from her grasp. Yanked off balance, she nearly fell, then straightened quickly.

The double charge had missed Bleeker's hip by a scant inch or so. His mouth was a flinty seam of rage as he pulled back a hamlike hand as if to strike her—then let it drop. His attention swiveled to the stranger as he pulled up in the yard.

"What's your business, pilgrim?" Croy Bleeker said harshly.

"With you, if you be Mr. Halsted."

The man's voice was lazy and summer-soft. He showed no more interest in the situation than if he'd intruded on a domestic fracas, as perhaps he thought was the case. He sat his roan horse at utter ease, hands crossed on the pommel.

Yet—he might be an ally.

"*Sogt av hustran!*" Kjerstin said quickly, then made herself speak carefully. "That's my husband . . . Anders Halsted is. This is not him."

"Doubted it was, ma'am," the stranger said mildly. "Not by thirty year, anyway. Had it this Halsted's a young man. He about, your husband?"

"No, no."

"This ain't your pappy, I take it."

"I'm Croy Bleeker," growled the rancher. "And you're on my range, mister. I'll say it once more, what's your business?"

"Name's Tom Kiskaddon. My business is with this Halsted man. Mind if I light down?"

He looked the question at Kjerstin, and remembering the custom of the country now, she nodded quickly. "*Ja*, please."

The man called Tom Kiskaddon stepped out of his saddle. He was on the short side, but very stocky and wiry. His square face was as dark and wooden as those of Indians she had seen; his straight black hair was streaked with gray, though he did not look over forty. His denim pants and duck jacket were chalky with wear and dust; his saddle and other gear looked well-worn.

His glance shuttled to Bleeker and back to Kjerstin. "Seems I have walked into something here. Would you be telling me what it is, ma'am?"

Bleeker threw the shotgun aside and suddenly palmed his big revolver out of its holster. "You walked into something all right, Texas. That's where you're from, ain't it?"

"Mr. Bleeker," Tom Kiskaddon said slowly, "man pulls a hogleg on me, he better be minded to use it."

"I'm minded, all right. First you answer up."

"I am from most any place you can name, but none of 'em's places where a man fetches a rough hand to any woman ain't his wife."

"I ain't set on harming no woman. But these snorkies is squatting on my land and I mean to move 'em off. You a cowman? Speak up!"

"Been that. Been a lot of things."

"We homestead here!" Kjerstin said hotly. "He has no right to do this. You, maybe you a lawman?"

"Been a lot of things. I have worn a badge in my time."

"Then what you are here," Croy Bleeker said softly, "is smack in the middle where there's no place for you. So what you do, you get on that nag and get packing."

Kiskaddon shook his head. "I got business to settle with Anders Halsted. When's he due back, ma'am, you know?"

"Texas—" Bleeker tramped over to the newcomer, sticking the gun almost in his face. "You just don't listen when a man talks." He reached out, lifted Kiskaddon's gun from its holster and shoved it in his own belt. "I ain't wasting no more time. Get in that shack."

"What for?"

"I tell you what for. This rat's nest is gonna get burned up, outsheds first. You and the woman will stay in the house till I have fired everything on the place. You stick your face outen that shack before I say, I will put a bullet in you. You get that all right?"

Kiskaddon gave a slight, wry shrug. But there was a feel, suddenly, of coiled violence about him, Kjerstin thought. No, there was more than that. There was a smell of danger. Yet he turned without a word and headed for the house. Bleeker motioned with his gun and Kjerstin, numbed by the arrogant and roughshod brutality of this old man, followed the Texan.

At the doorway, Kiskaddon stepped aside and removed his hat, courteously indicating that Kjerstin should go in first. She did, and he entered behind her. What came next was so swift and furious that it was over almost before she knew what was happening.

Anders, himself a sturdy six-footer, had set the doorway so that a normally tall man might enter without ducking his head. Kiskaddon walked through easily; Bleeker, towering inches above six feet, deeply inclined his head and shoulders as he entered. In that instant, while Bleeker's eyes were bent down, Kiskaddon wheeled, slapping his hat across Bleeker's face. A startled grunt left the rancher; he momentarily froze in a half-stooped position. Then Kiskaddon's fist slammed into his belly like a mule's kick.

As Bleeker doubled over, Kiskaddon's other hand siezed his gun and twisted it away, then chopped it in a short savage arc that ended against Bleeker's temple. The big man swayed forward; Kiskaddon moved aside and let him crash to the floor.

Kiskaddon said, "Bring me a dipper of water, ma'am, if you'll be so kind," as he bent and caught Bleeker by the shoulder and turned him over. Pulling his gun from Bleeker's belt now, he stepped back.

Kjerstin handed him the dipper. Kiskaddon tipped it, dribbling water slowly over Bleeker's face. The rancher stirred, blinked, groaned, and finally staggered to his feet. He had to grab at the wall for support; he wiped a hand over his face and brought his eyes to focus.

"I'm going . . . to kill you . . . for that . . . pilgrim," he said, dredging the words up with a grunt.

"Drag it," Kiskaddon murmured. "Go on, clear out before I light a match to your britches."

Moments later, as they stood in the yard watching Bleeker ride slowly back toward the Notch, Kjerstin still felt an amazement touched by awe and bewilderment. Surely a man like Bleeker had never been treated like that, spoken to like that, in his life. She looked at Tom Kiskaddon.

"*Tack så mycket!* I must thank you so much."

"Nothing, ma'am. I don't cotton to a man waving a gun under my nose."

"But now, I think, maybe you better watch out for him. He is very mad."

"Yes'm, that's why I took his Colt and saddle gun away from him. Anyways I don't aim to stay longer'n I need to conclude my business with Mr. Halsted. When you say he'll be back?"

Kjerstin explained why she couldn't be sure. "But you are welcome to stay till he comes, Mr. Kiskaddon. You are very welcome."

"Thanks. I'll just make camp under them oaks yonder."

"*Ja*, and I will make you a good supper."

Kiskaddon protested; he seemed oddly ill at ease, as if reluctant to accept this hospitality, and she wondered about that. But she overrode his objection and went into the house to prepare the meal. When it was ready, she called him, and he came tramping out of the oak grove, washed up, and took a place at the table. He ate his way silently and hungrily through second helpings, as if he hadn't eaten well in a long time.

Something about the man made Kjerstin vaguely uneasy. Maybe it was his face, so guarded and still, or that leashed tension she sensed in him. He made only the briefest of responses to anything she said, otherwise speaking not at all. It was bad form to ask a man his business, she knew, but asked anyway.

"What you want to see Anders for? Maybe I can help, eh?"

"No, ma'am."

So much for that. "You been a cowman, mister? And a lawman?"

"Yes'm."

"What else you been?"

"Army scout, prospector, stage driver, shotgun guard, bounty hunter, detective for a cattleman's association, soldier in the war."

Again, it seemed, that was that. Like Anders, like many men in the west, this Tom Kiskaddon had known many occupations. But most of the things he mentioned marked him as not only a man of action, but one inclined toward violence and danger. From his handling of Croy Bleeker, she knew he could handle such jobs very well.

She made idle talk, telling him of their plans for the farm, telling how Anders had put up the cabin almost single-handed (with her help), cutting and snaking logs out of the pine-crowned heights around the valley, and how they had planned the house so that additions could be made as their family grew.

"It is very lonely here, but it is better for me when the baby comes, eh? Anders, he says we are so far from anywhere, we must build a school for the kids. We will, too, if that Mr. Bleeker lets us alone."

Kiskaddon finished his coffee, scraped back his chair

and stood up. "Thank you for the supper." He moved to the door and paused there, giving her a look out of those chill eyes. "You don't understand men like him. Bleeker."

"No, mister. He wants more than a man needs. But maybe you understand, eh?"

"I reckon I do. My pappy is like him. They tamed the country so people like you can live it safe."

Her brow puckered. "Safe—from people like him?"

"You got a point. But they fought for the land."

"So will we, if we must."

"Well, that's fair."

He sounded totally indifferent; he started out the door and she spoke sharply, halting him. "Mr. Kiskaddon. You come a long way to see my husband—is it so?"

"Yes, ma'am."

"But why?"

Again that straight look of his; again that feel of coiled danger in the man. But now, somehow, it chilled her to the bone. "Why," he said softly, "you might call it a point of honor. It has got to be satisfied."

For a moment, after he went out, Kjerstin stared at the doorway then rose and cleared the table. She cleaned up quickly and prepared for bed, unbraiding her hair and letting it down, slipping into her long flannel nightgown. Twilight was fading into dusk as she barred the door and extinguished the lamp.

The darkness was warm and oppressive, but she still felt cold. Going to the window, she gazed out at the moonlit valley, rubbing her crossed arms. How vast and empty-seeming this country was. At least on the remote mountain farm where she'd grown up, there'd been people, father and mother and three sisters. Kjerstin, though the oldest of them, had been the last to wed. For her there had never been anyone but Anders Halsted, who had grown up on a neighboring farm and had gone to America six years ago. There had been promises and letters, though her letters to him were often months catching up. It had been five years before her patience and belief were rewarded and Anders had sent for her. All was so new and strange in this land, even with Anders waiting for her when she came off the boat, always at her side during the long journey by train and stage across a continent.

She regretted none of it. Fear and loneliness there were sometimes, but these were to be conquered, and in the doing, courage and the strength to go on could be found.

The fear she felt tonight was very different. It was a nameless chill that she couldn't think how to fight. This Tom Kiskaddon did not know her husband, yet had come far looking for him, and for a reason he was unwilling to name. She realized how little, really, she knew of Anders' life during those five years of separation. His letters had kept to generalities. He had done well in the new land, but that was only to be expected; he was strong, clever, hard-working and a natural leader, and such men made their way quickly. Kjerstin was proud of her man, yet an uneasy doubt she'd never known was seeded in her. What had happened, what had he done, to bring this stranger looking for him?

She slipped into bed, but sleep did not come. Now and again, turning restlessly, she threw an arm across the empty space beside her that Anders, warm and solid and comforting, usually occupied in the bed he had brought here on a horse drag, clear from Indian Grove thirty miles away where they had purchased their supplies.

Worried as she was, the weariness of her body soon overcame her mind. She was falling into a black cotton of sleep when the noise came—a light tap at the door, then a harder one.

She sat bolt upright, trembling.

"*Käresta?* Are you awake?"

For a confused moment she thought she was dreaming, then Anders spoke again. Hurrying to the door, Kjerstin flung the bar off its brackets, swung the door open and was in his arms, feeling his solid bulk and the roughness of his beard. Quickly she pulled him inside and shut the door.

"I was nearly home when dark came," Anders said, "so I figure there is no need to camp out." He fumbled his way toward the table. "Here, I'll light the lamp. . . ."

"No! Do not make a light. Listen, I must tell you. . . ."

Even as the words left her, the door was thrust open abruptly and moonlight spilled into the room. Kiskaddon stood on the threshold, a glint of metal in his fist. He heard Anders ride in, Kjerstin thought sinkingly.

"Don't make a wrong move, Halsted. I can see you good enough and I got a gun on you."

"Who are you?" Anders demanded. "What you want?"

"You'll know directly. Light up that lamp and we'll talk."

Kjerstin stood numbly as Anders struck a match and the lamp's saffron glow spread through the room. Anders frowned at the Texan, then at his wife. "This man . . . you knew he was here?"

"Tell him, Miz Halsted," murmured Kiskaddon.

She managed a patchy explanation, mixing Swedish words with English in her agitation.

"So," Anders nodded, still frowning. "I thank you for helping her. But what is it you want with me? I never see you before."

Kiskaddon advanced slowly into the room, not taking his eyes off Anders as he reached inside his coat and pulled out a worn leather wallet which he tossed onto the table. Anders picked up the wallet and opened it, producing a faded photograph. It was, Kjerstin saw, the portrait of a smiling youth wearing range clothes and posed stiffly against some studio scenery of painted fence and trees.

"Russ Kiskaddon," said Anders. "I knew him in Texas. He died—"

"—at a river crossing," Kiskaddon cut in harshly. "That tell you enough?"

Anders dropped picture and wallet on the table. "Maybe it tells me why you're here. You want to find out more about how your brother died, eh? It don't tell me why you point a gun at me."

Kiskaddon's shoulders hunched as if he were a cat preparing to spring. He was a very direct man, used to making snap decisions. "First you tell me how Russ died. Your story, Halsted."

"I was trail-bossing the Rafter J herd from Texas to Abilene in Kansas," Anders said slowly. "At the crossing on the Red River, the water was high. Your brother was helping push cows down the dugway into the river. The lead steer, he turned back, got the others milling in the middle of the river. Your brother and some of the other men tried to wedge their ponies on the flank to turn the mill. Russ Kiskaddon and his animal went down in it.

Another man pulled him out, but Russ had been gored in the belly. I am sorry, Kiskaddon. A man on trail takes his chances, your brother with the rest. That is all."

"It ain't all," Kiskaddon said in an iron voice. "Your cook was a doctor of sorts, got the boy patched up, told you moving him 'ud be the death of him. That didn't count for shucks with you, seeing you was bound to put the first herd of the season into Abilene, fetch the best prices. Couple of the crew offered to camp behind with the kid till he was well enough to go on. You wouldn't have that neither, said you was undermanned already and needed every man to finish up the drive. The kid would have to ride in the cook's wagon."

"That is not—"

"You leave me finish. When your crew balked at that, you forced 'em on at gunpoint. The drive went on with my brother in the wagon jolting up and down till he hemorrhaged. You killed him, Halsted, same as if you put a gun to his head!"

"No," said Anders. "I am not a man to do that. Your brother was dead when pulled from the river. The rest of it is not true. So, I think, it was Quint Bailey who told you a lie."

"It was our old pappy he told. Our folks got a place on the Nueces and Quint brung Russ's belongings there. I was way up north and it was most of a year 'fore I got home for a visit and got the story from Pappy. Took me damn near again as long to run you down, Halsted. You quit the Rafter J after that drive and then dropped out o' sight. But I am an old hand on cold trails."

"I did not try to hide my trail," Anders said stiffly. "I had other things to do, a new life to make. My savings I drew from the bank in Kansas City, I went east to meet a girl promised to me, to marry her and bring her here and—"

"Yeh, I know all that. What it boils down to is you was lying or Quint Bailey was. Now why would he?"

"He was drinking on the drive. When I took the whiskey away from him, he made trouble. I had to beat him up to put him in line. After that he was very mean. This, I think, is why he lied to your father." Anders shook his head wryly. "He volunteered to take Russ' things to his people, as he said he knew them. This I agreed to, and I think it was a mistake, eh?"

"Maybe that wa'n't your only mistake, mister," Kiskaddon murmured. "The Baileys and the Kiskaddons neighbored a long time. Quint and me grew up together. He was allus a right sort."

"Maybe," Anders said dryly, "but that was when you was kids, and men change, eh?"

"You saying he lied to get me on your ass? That is what it comes down to."

"I think that is it. I have heard of you, Kiskaddon. Your name is known, and Russ would boast of you. He was proud of his brother."

"We was damn close. Our people is raised that way. One comes to harm, it's an eye for an eye. But I pull iron on a man, I want to be sure of him. You can't take back a bullet. That is why we are talking. But it will take a damn sight more'n words from you to convince me, mister."

"Maybe, then, you could of found other men was on that drive. They would tell you the same."

"Didn't figure that was called for. I trusted Quint Bailey's word." Kiskaddon paused, then said grudgingly, "You ain't the kind o' man I expected. I have seen your place here and have met your fine wife. I have got to own I ain't sure no more."

"So, then?"

"Ain't nothing for it but to do like you said. We have got to hunt up others who was on that drive and see what they say. We will start out in the morning."

Anders shook his head. "Not 'we', mister. It is a long way to the Rafter J in Texas and I have crops to get in and much work to do on the place before winter. Also, I cannot leave my wife. So you will ride alone to find the truth."

Kiskaddon's eyes narrowed wickedly. "I ain't offering you no choice, Halsted. Think I'll give you a chance to skip out of the country? You are coming with me."

Kjerstin watched Anders' face harden into that quiet, mulish set that she knew. Her dread crowded deeper, knowing what his answer would be.

They were all startled by the voice at the door.

"You stand like you are, Texas. I got a gun square on your back."

It was the voice of Croy Bleeker, coming out of the night through the open door behind Kiskaddon. For a scared moment Kjerstin peered against the moon-webbed outer dark till she made out the man's hulk. He had come very quietly; he must have left his horse a ways off. But did he have a gun? She couldn't be sure.

As if she'd asked the question aloud, Bleeker grated, "There's a line shack of mine ain't far off. Borrowed the gun there. You can believe it, Texas."

Kiskaddon's wiry body tensed as if he were ready to take a chance and wheel against the drop. But he didn't.

Bleeker moved forward into the light now, a rifle in his hands. The side of his face wore a swollen welt where

Kiskaddon had struck him. "I got business with you too, Halsted—" His voice grated like a rusty saw. "It will get settled tonight for good."

Without warning, he swept the rifle up and smashed its stock against Kiskaddon's skull. The Texan plunged down on his face.

Even as Kiskaddon was falling, Anders scooped up the heavy lamp next to his hand and hurled it swiftly and strongly, as a man would throw a ball or a rock overhand, at Bleeker. The lamp's weighted base struck his shoulder with an impact that knocked Bleeker reeling. Floundering wildly off balance, he slammed against the wall.

Kiskaddon's pistol had skidded almost by Kjerstin's foot. She needed only to pick it up and double-thumb it to cock. This she did so quickly, almost unthinkingly, that Bleeker had only half-straightened up, his rifle pointed awkwardly down, before she had it leveled on him.

"Drop the gun, mister! I will shoot!"

Croy Bleeker let it drop. He rubbed his bruised shoulder, glowering.

"So," Anders said. "I think it is time we are straight with each other, Bleeker. They say a man can shoot a trespasser. Should I tell my wife to shoot you?"

"Do it and be damned to you."

Anders shook his head. "I don't understand you much, mister. But I think you don't understand us at all." He nodded at Kiskaddon. "No more than this one does."

Kiskaddon groaned, dragged himself to a sitting position, and rubbed the back of his head. A ribbon of blazing coal oil had sprayed across the packed-clay floor from the lamp, which now lay on its side with the glass chimney shattered. In the light from the fire it made the two men's eyes were like nail heads heated to a glow as they watched Anders.

"It would be easy to do," Anders said steadily. "But we are not like you men. You, Bleeker. You can come again and again here, even bring men to help you, but you cannot scare us off; we will not run. We will fight you. So then, maybe you or some of your men will die. Or you will kill both of us. Look at it, Bleeker. Are you ready to do that?"

Bleeker scowled. "I can burn your goddamn place and run you out——"

"But maybe you will kill us doing it. And if you do not kill us, we will be back. Finally, you will have to kill us—or we will kill you when you try. I say it again, Bleeker . . . *look at it.*"

Anders moved over to Kjerstin now and took the gun from her hand. He held it out to Kiskaddon, who slowly took it and got to his feet.

"To you I say the same," Anders told him. "If I do not go with you like you say, you can only do one thing. Can you do it, mister?"

"You're crazy!" Croy Bleeker spat. "By Christ, you got to be!"

"Well," Anders said calmly, "if I am wrong, I give you the chance to show us." He pointed at Bleeker's rifle. "There it is. Pick it up. You will never have a better chance—I will never give you one."

A rush of protest swelled in Kjerstin's throat. But she kept silent, watching Bleeker, and saw a crack of uncertainty, then a mounting, baffled anger, break over his craggy face. Slowly now he picked up the rifle and fingered it, eying Anders.

Then Croy Bleeker said with a savage disgust, "Ah-h-h——" and turned, tramping out the door.

Both Halsteds looked at Kiskaddon now.

He gave that slight, wry shrug of his, then holstered his gun. "I reckon that says it all, says the kind of man you are for sure. But you took a long chance with Bleeker right then, mister. He has lived by the gun in his time."

Anders nodded. "Yes, it was a chance. But worth the taking. He has lived by the gun, but he is not a killer, no more than you are. Maybe, I thought, if I could make the man look at all of it at once, see it for what it would mean, it would not have to happen. And now I think it will not. There is—I do not know how to say all of this—but when men are not all bad, not sick with badness, there is an honor in them."

"Yeh." Kiskaddon rubbed his jaw. "Honor. It's a funny thing. Brought me a far ways just to find you."

"Your 'point of honor,'" said Kjerstin. "*Ja*, it brought you a long way, mister. And for nothing, I think."

For the first time she saw Kiskaddon smile.

"No, ma'am," he said, "not for nothing. Not when it's been satisfied."

THE WAR AT PEACEVILLE

The trail town made a small break in the sweep of prairie. A shipping point for Texas cattle, it nestled in a crook of the Spanish River, and they called it Peaceville. However, the irony of the name failed to tickle even the acidly tolerant humor of Dr. Mordaunt Stern, whose inveterate motto was *Illegitimi non carborundum*: Don't let the bastards wear you down.

Dr. Stern, a plumpish man with a cherubic face and a nimbus of white hair that circled his head like a spurious halo, was sitting this afternoon in one of Peaceville's dozen saloons, talking things over with Regis O'Herlihy, who owned the general mercantile store, and Muley Foran, the mild-mannered livery barn proprietor and town marshal.

Having lubricated their faculties with several eye-openers, the three friends agreed without difficulty on the root of the town's problem: it was split down the middle. On the one side were Jess Renard and his gambler colleagues who promoted a wide open town with its inevitable cynosure for lawless elements and constant hoorawing by wild trail hands. On the other side were the merchants, professional men, honest saloon keepers and the settlers who patronized them, people who wanted to see schools, churches, and ladies' aid societies come to Peaceville. As conditions stood, the community's name made it a laughing stock across the whole of Kansas. That had been true even before Huck Winters, a town marshal who'd kept things generally well in hand, had been shot from a dark alley by an unknown assailant a month ago.

"Arragh, we know what the trouble is," observed Regis O'Herlihy, a gaunt, salty-tongued man in a shapeless black suit. "Question is, what do we do about it?"

Both he and Dr. Stern looked at little Muley Foran, whose faded eyes widened owlishly. "Now don't you men go blaming me none. I ain't no Huck Winters. I jist agreed to wear this hunk o' tin till we get poor ole Huck replaced."

"Well," Doc said sourly, "we sure as hell need more than token authority behind that badge. War has come to Peaceville, boys, and being on the side of angels is of no use unless you have got Gabriel to lead 'em."

Standing, Doc rammed his hands in his hip pockets and sauntered to the batwing doors, scowling out at the street. He was no fist-or-gun man himself. And Regis O'Herlihy, whose big leonine face held the stubborn fearlessness of a man who'd come up the hard way, was old and stiff with arthritis.

A smell of hot dust lifted off the street as a man on a lean nag rode down it and dismounted before the saloon. Doc stared at him with interest as he tied up and tramped onto the porch.

He drawled, "Aftuhnoon," as Doc stepped aside to let him enter. He was built like a blacksmith, a tall bull-shouldered man with a broad, cheerful, weather-beaten face partly hidden by scruffy black whiskers. The hair of his temples was touched with little devil's horns of white, though he probably wasn't over thirty. Despite his size, he was quick and light on his feet.

As the newcomer crossed to the bar, Doc went briskly back to the table where his companions sat. "How do you size that fellow?" he asked in a conspiratorial whisper.

"Stranger," said Muley Foran.

"Has a 'Big Fifty' in his saddle boot," said Doc. "Clothes all stained with grease and blood. Hide hunter, looks like, just off the prairie."

"Can a man be asking what cooks under your thatch, Mordaunt?" demanded O'Herlihy.

Before Doc could reply, the batwing doors parted again and Keno Paul, one of the dealers from Renard's Keno House, came in and moved a little unsteadily to the bar, raising a finger for whiskey. Keno Paul was a slender frock-coated fellow noted for being moody and taciturn and unapproachable except when drink brought out his other nature, that of a congenital troublemaker. The wicked interest with which he now regarded the big stranger indicated that he was carrying a snootful.

Rory, the barkeep, brought him a bottle and glass. Keno Paul poured himself a drink, then said, "Have a snort with me, pilgrim? Howsabout it?" And slid the bottle of whiskey down the bar. It stopped just short of the big man's elbow.

"Thank you, suh, no," the buffalo hunter said in a soft Southern voice. "I don't drink whiskey." He nodded toward his own glass. "Beer now, that sets light on a man's liver."

"You won't drink with me, huh?"

"No, suh, begging your pardon."

"Maybe," Keno Paul suggested gently, "you are looking for trouble, Mac?"

Rory reached under his bar for the bung starter he kept close at hand, whereupon Keno Paul stepped swiftly away from the bar, grinning. He barely glanced at Rory, just held a wicked eye on the stranger.

"Now what would you do, Mac," he said softly, "if I just *insisted—*"

As he spoke, his hand brushed back his frock coat and settled on the butt of a holstered gun.

Another man might have hesitated; the stranger didn't. Quick as thought he swept up the bottle of whiskey in one huge hand and threw it, hitting Keno Paul in the chest so hard he staggered back. For a moment he was dumbfounded; then he swore and yanked out his gun. But the stranger was still in motion, following up the bottle with three long strides toward Keno Paul. He wrenched the gun from the dealer's hand, tossed it on the bar, caught him by the neck with one hand, swung him in a complete circle and let go. The bar brought Keno Paul up with a crash.

He whirled out from the bar, face twisted with rage, and swung a long, booted leg up in a vicious kick. The big man turned so the kick took him high on the outer thigh, then seized a handful of Keno Paul's pleated white shirt and swung a sledgelike fist to his jaw. The dealer sagged upright in his grasp and the stranger let go, dropping him limply to the floor.

The big man walked back to his beer and finished it in a swallow, leaning an elbow on the bar with the relaxed poise of one who'd just performed an unpleasant but minor chore. Yet Doc noted the grooves of tension along his jaw; the little white devil's horns above his temples which seemed to bristle slightly.

Rory laid his bung starter on the bar, then came around with a pail of water. He poured it over Keno Paul, who sat up spluttering, then climbed painfully to his feet. Rory quietly set down the pail, handed the dealer his gun, and picked up his bung starter, slapping it gently against his palm as he stood between Keno Paul and the stranger. The dealer glared at him, then turned without a word and stamped out.

Doc walked over to the stranger. "Handily done, young man. Would you do my friends and me the honor of joining us in a glass?"

"I don't take whiskey, suh."

"So I noticed. Another beer for this gentleman, Rory."

Doc introduced himself and his companions. The big man shook hands all around, and said his name was Ox Rhiannon. He had been with a party of buffalo hunters who had just split up after selling a sizable harvest of hides. Having a good-sized poke in his jeans and wanting to loaf for a few weeks, Rhiannon had decided to sojourn in Peaceville till his fiddle-foot got itching again.

"Yours is a lively profession at present," Doc observed, "but a man should give an eye to his future. In five years or less, the big herds will be hunted out."

"Yes, suh," Ox Rhiannon agreed. "But I figure by cutting it fine I will have saved enough in a couple years to start a horse ranch, which is what I have an eye to."

"Well now, you don't want to cut it too fine. You seem a capable fellow; I hate to see talent like yours going to waste. What would you say to a position that pays a hundred dollars a month, plus room and board and other expenses?"

"It has a choice ring to it. What is the position?"

Doc explained the town's need for a competent peace officer, one not allied by sympathy or occupation to the cattle drovers. Of course Rhiannon's appointment would be subject to endorsement by the town council, but since three of its five members were Regis O'Herlihy, Muley Foran and Doc himself—

The big man was already shaking his head.

"Don't be so hasty, young man," Doc said with some asperity. "You might at least give the offer due consideration."

"I have considered, suh. Thank you for the beer. Gentlemen—" Ox Rhiannon gave them a courteous nod and walked out.

"A pity," said O'Herlihy. "I thought we were downwind of a damn likely prospect in that young Cuchulain."

"We still are," said Doc. "He will be around awhile, and that'll give me time to work on and overcome his reluctance."

"Arragh, Mordaunt, ye sound determined."

"Well," Muley Foran said worriedly, "you boys know that toting this here badge has give me a case of fluttering fantods and I am looking to part company with it shortly. In fact I am declaring my resignation effective as of midnight a week from today."

Business being slow that afternoon, Doc dropped into Regis O'Herlihy's store for a visit with the proprietor. Here he found Ox Rhiannon in animated conversation with O'Herlihy's daughter, Molly. If it hadn't been for the hide hunter's unmistakable size, Doc would have been hard put to recognize him. Rhiannon wore a new suit, still fold-wrinkled from the shelf, he was cleanshaven and no doubt fresh from a bath. Seeing him with pretty Molly gave a positive uplift to Doc's crafty heart. Just possibly a means of persuasion was nearer at hand than he'd realized. Holding his face grave and composed, Doc said a polite hello and asked Molly if her father were about.

Before she could reply, O'Herlihy came out of the back room. His look of non-professional affability at sight of Doc altered to one just short of cold disapproval, seeing his daughter and the hide hunter standing in rather confidential proximity.

"Would you be wanting to make a purchase, Mr. Rhiannon?" he asked pointedly.

Slightly disconcerted, Rhiannon said, "Er, well, I would like to look at some guns, suh."

O'Herlihy motioned toward the gun case, and Rhiannon stepped over to it. The two older men began chatting; then Riannon turned to them with a gun he'd taken from the case. "Pardon, suh. Is this one of those new center-fire weapons I have heard tell of?"

"Hm? Oh. Oh, yes." O'Herlihy took the gun from him. "Haven't seen one of these, have you, Mordaunt? A '72 model Colt's .45, first of its kind in town."

"What's special about it?" Doc asked.

"Oh, a matter of ballistics." O'Herlihy displayed a pardonable pride in having an edge on the learned Doc in a technical matter. "Till now, all revolving weapons have been rim-fire, with a disadvantage in accuracy as opposed to this new center-fire. When the firing pin hits the center of the primer, the powder is exploded with even force, so hurling the bullet more true."

"Is this one for sale, suh?" Rhiannon asked.

"Afraid not. I merely put it out for display. Want to get rid of my old stock in handguns before ordering the improved model in quantity. Sent East for this one on special order by a friend of yours, Keno Paul, and it just arrived. He hasn't called for it yet."

"Friend?" Rhiannon scratched his head. "I don't recollect—"

"The party you messed up in Rory's this morning," said Doc.

Rhiannon nodded, eying the gun regretfully. "A good weapon should be carried by a good man." He turned to Miss O'Herlihy. "Ma'am, I hope you won't find it abrupt of me, but I would be obliged for the honor of your company on a buggy drive this afternoon."

O'Herlihy looked shocked; then he reddened with anger. "Young man, it is not the way even in Peaceville to make overtures to a young woman within five minutes of meeting her. And especially it's not to my daughter a man will be making such—"

Doc took a light grip on the storekeeper's arm. "Regis, I'd like a professional word with you. In private."

They stepped into the back room, and O'Herlihy demanded truculently, "Well?"

"Think, Regis. If Molly will lend a hand, we may have the means to persuade that broth of a lad to fill the marshal's shoes."

"Arragh! Are ye suggesting I lend my own flesh and blood to such an end?"

"Want to see the town made a safe place for her, don't you? If female charms will turn the trick, and perhaps they're all that will, it's a small matter next to the benefit to be reaped. Anyway—" Doc smiled "—an 'ox' this Rhiannon may be where the fair sex is concerned, but his manners show he comes of good stock."

It took five minutes of patient argument to secure O'Herlihy's reluctant agreement. He and Doc returned to the front of the store where Rhiannon was still conversing, a little abashedly now, with Molly.

O'Herlihy cleared his throat. "My dear, the doctor has pointed out to me that you're a bit peaked with all this clerking and bookkeeping. It might be well for ye to take an outing this afternoon with Mr. Rhiannon, as he suggested."

Rhiannon, even more disconcerted by this about-face, said awkwardly, "Will you do me the honor, Miss O'Herlihy?"

Molly's blue eyes sparkled; Doc guessed that she suspected what was up and that it tickled her Irish sense of mischief. She demurely lowered her lashes. "I would be most pleased. . . ."

At the end of a week, however, Doc's goal seemed no nearer its realization. Having taken a room at the hotel, Ox Rhiannon courted Molly O'Herlihy in the evenings, slept late every morning, and spent his afternoons playing checkers with Muley Foran. Meantime he politely refused to give in to Molly's subtle cajoling and Doc's persuasive eloquence.

On Saturday evening, Doc had just left the New York Cafe and was crossing the street, pausing to light his after-dinner cigar, when a gang of hard-riding trail hands came barreling into town for a night's whoop-up, firing off their six-shooters. Doc was compelled to the indignity of a stumbling run to the street's far side, where he found that he'd lost his cigar and that his trousers were splattered with mud.

After a few choice epithets, he continued toward his office and quarters, seething with bitterness toward Ox Rhiannon. As he drew abreast of O'Herlihy's store, he saw the object of his wrath standing in the shadow of the store's wooden awning with Molly. He appeared to be having heated words with her.

"You are quite right, Mr. Rhiannon," Doc heard the girl say icily. "A man should certainly move on if he finds nothing worth staying for. Good night!"

She went into the store, and Ox Rhiannon left the porch and started down the street, his strides long and angry. Doc caught up and fell in step beside him, presently saying mildly, "Fight?"

"Doc, I cannot claim to understand women."

Doc nodded sourly, digging out another cigar. "Uh-huh. Welcome to the club."

"Why in the devil must they turn everything a man says back on him? I sort of hinted that I might be leaving Peaceville soon as there was nothing for me here. This, mind you, only to lead up to a proposal of marriage so that we might leave together. She did not give me a chance to say so."

"Strange creatures, women," Doc agreed blandly, touching a match to his cigar. Privately he guessed that Ox had broached the matter oxily. "Seems to me, though, you're overlooking prospects right under your nose."

"Doc, I would be obliged if you do not grease that axle again. Can I buy you a drink?"

Doc found the suggestion commendable, and the two of them swung into the nearest saloon, the First Chance.

Once inside the thinly crowded room, Doc recalled that this was one of Jess Renard's places. He hesitated, then signaled the bartender for whiskey, being old and wise enough not to carry politics into his drinking.

Warmed by the glow of two quick ones, he decided to put the question point-blank, "Ox, why won't you take the marshal's job?"

Rhiannon was brooding into his glass of beer. He was silent for a half-minute, then said without raising his eyes, "When I wasn't much more than a kid, I served a spell in prison. Manslaughter. I fought with a man and killed him with my bare hands. I have a temper and am scared of it and of what might happen if I took a job that demands the use of force."

"You won't find out by running away from it."

"Doc, remember that Keno Paul fellow the other day? If I had been a little madder, I'd have broken his neck for him—"

"Ain't that interesting."

The mocking voice brought both men around. Keno Paul was standing there, assured and cocky and smiling wickedly. The skirt of his frock coat was swept back from his hip, where the new center-fire Colt nestled. "Well," he said ominously, "I have been thinking of calling you out, Mac. It will give you a chance to finish the job."

Rhiannon shook his head. "Forget it. Have a drink."

"I made you that offer, as I recall. If I turn you down, is it worth a fight?"

"No. Forget it."

"Well then, how is your mother?"

"What?"

"She must come from fine gutter stock to spawn a yellow dog like you."

Obviously expecting Rhiannon to respond as he did, Keno Paul rolled back with the blow, but it was enough to knock him on his back. He got slowly to his feet, holding a handkerchief to his bleeding nose. "Have you got a gun?" he asked.

"You can see I am not armed."

"I'll be back in fifteen minutes. See that you are." Keno Paul turned and walked out of the saloon.

Rhiannon swiped a hand across his jaw, then settled a bitter stare on Doc. "All right. He wanted me to do that, and I'm a damn fool for going along."

"And maybe a dead one, which is more important. How well do you handle a sidearm?"

"I teethed on one. But I don't own one now and I'll not use one."

"Then we'd better move elsewhere."

Rhiannon's jaw shelved out; he shook his head. Doc gave him a baffled look, then signaled for two more drinks, but Rhiannon did not touch his, only waited.

About fifteen minutes later a slim, frock-coated figure entered the place, but it wasn't Keno Paul. Jess Renard, a pale, debonair, ghost of a man who was tastefully dressed and carried a silver-headed walking stick, swung his dark stare around the room, then came over to Doc and Rhiannon.

"Mr. Rhiannon? I am Renard. I am here to speak of a misunderstanding between you and my man, Keno Paul. I have already spoken to him."

"What rock did you discover his intentions under?" Doc asked with quiet malice.

"He was boasting of them; such matters have a way of reaching my ears quickly, Doctor." Renard flashed a surprisingly wolfish smile; it was like a mask dropping. "Keno has behaved intemperately with your friend, I fear."

"Not really," said Doc. "He didn't hit below the knees even once."

"Well, I've told him not to trouble Mr. Rhiannon further. Shall we let the matter drop?" Renard lowered his voice. "Just one thing, Doctor. I understand the town council wants to pin a badge on this young husky."

"What if we do?"

"He might find it inadvisable to accept." Renard shuttled his glance to Rhiannon. "Nothing personal, my friend, just a word to the wise. You look like a sensible fellow."

"I like to think I'm that, suh," Rhiannon murmured. "But would like you to make the sense of it clear to me."

"Oh, I'm sure you're well aware of the whys and wherefores—the good doctor would have seen to that. And I trust there'll be no necessity for my making them clearer still. That, of course, will depend entirely on you. Gentlemen!" Renard tapped his hat brim with the walking stick, then turned and went out.

Rhiannon raised his glass of beer, drained it and set it down. Doc wisely said nothing. After a full minute, Ox Rhiannon said quietly, "Doc, I do not like the cut of this Mr. Renard or his heel dog. I don't like people who think they can beat any game all the way all the time. People like that should be helped along on their ride to a fall."

Doc shrugged. "You know how you can best do that. I've told you often enough."

Rhiannon scrubbed a hand slowly over his face. "Doc, I don't know. I just don't know. Give me a spell to think on it. . . ."

It was nearly midnight when the two men, not too unsteadily, left the First Chance. A minute or so before they exited the place, they'd heard the racketing echo of a shot down the street, but had attached no importance to it. Now, seeing a knot of men gather at the mouth of the alley between the gunsmith's and the hotel, they headed curiously that way. A man came hurrying to meet them.

"Doc, you better get over there quick. Muley Foran has been shot and he's bad off, looks like. . . ."

Doc shoved through the crowd and dropped to one knee by his friend. Muley lay on his back, his gun undrawn. After a cursory examination, Doc snapped, "He's alive, and that's about all. Here, Ox, and you, Charley, lend a hand; get him over to my office."

Doc went ahead to get things in readiness. Spectators tagged along; he testily told them to clear out, except for Rhiannon. With Ox's assistance, he set to digging the lead out of Muley, then cleaned and dressed the wound. Afterward, as he washed his hands, Doc said, "That is all we can do for him, but it should be enough."

"Shot in the back," Rhiannon said softly. "So close his coat was powder-burned. Is that how your Marshal Winters got it?"

"Just so," Doc said wearily. "From a dark alley while making his rounds. We can't be sure till Muley regains consciousness, but it's ten to one he didn't see his assailant's face." A hard bitterness etched his voice. "Muley was no threat as a marshal. He was just expendable."

"As a warning, I would say."

"Just so. Renard wanted to be sure you got his message."

Rhiannon turned away, his jaw working.

"Yes, boy," Doc said gently, "you do that, you think on it, sleep on it." He tugged out his watch and stared at it. "It's just midnight. You know something? Muley's resignation as town marshal is now effective. . . ."

Doc didn't get much sleep himself, rising frequently during the night to check on his patient's condition. By morning Muley was conscious enough to briefly confirm that he'd never glimpsed the man who'd shot him. He was sweating in a high fever, and then he slept again. Doc was drifting into exhausted slumber on his lumpy office couch when a knock came at the door. He opened it to a raw blaze of sunlight, blinking groggily. Ox Rhiannon stood there, his "Big Fifty" Sharps rifle tucked under his arm.

"How's Muley?"

"In slightly better shape than I am," Doc snapped.

"Sorry, Doc. I have found something you will want to know about. . . ."

Doc was wide awake before Rhiannon had finished the brief telling, and then he said softly, exultantly, "That could just do it. How'd you like to pay a call on Mr. Renard?"

Rhiannon patted the Sharps. "I had hoped you would suggest it."

Doc splashed some water on his face, then pulled his coat on over his sleep-rumpled clothing. "Just one thing first, boy. . . ." He went to the pile of Muley's clothes, found the badge and held it up. "How about doing this right? We'll confirm your appointment later."

Rhiannon nodded resignedly.

Jess Renard's office was at the rear of the Keno House. The two men strode through the long gambling hall, ignoring the swamper who was cleaning up, and walked unceremoniously into the office. The owner was sitting at his desk in his shirt sleeves, studying a ledger before him. He looked up, eyes pinching at the corners.

"Doors are for knocking at as well as for opening, gentlemen." Renard's gaze touched the badge on Rhiannon's vest. "I take it this is an official visit? You've ignored my suggestion, Marshal."

"That suggestion was a big mistake," Rhiannon said gently. "Now, suh, I have one for you. Get up and walk out of here ahead of me."

Five minutes later, the three of them barged into Keno Paul's hotel room with a similar lack of ceremony. The dealer wheeled around from the commode mirror, hairbrush in hand.

"What the hell!"

"It seems," Renard said tightly, "that the doctor and *our new marshal* are curious as to your whereabouts last night at the time that Marshal Foran was shot."

Keno Paul's face veiled with a thin caution. "I ain't sure when that was."

"Between eleven-fifteen and eleven-thirty ought to cover it," said Doc. "Think hard."

"I reckon I was out back of the Keno House having a smoke. I took a break about that time."

"Can you prove it?" Rhiannon asked.

"Hell, the houseman who took over my game can tell you. Lenny Cates, it was. Ask him."

"Whoever saw you come and go," Doc said dryly, "hardly cuts ice on the pond. It won't account for your whereabouts during those fifteen minutes." He glanced at Renard. "Too bad you didn't prepare an alibi for him, Jess. But then you had no reason to believe he'd need one, did you?"

"I still don't," Renard said coldly. "He needn't prove a damned thing. If, on the basis of God knows what wild guess, you're accusing him of shooting Foran—and, I presume, me of ordering it done—you'll require evidence. Do you have it?"

"I think we have," Rhiannon murmured. Holding his rifle pointed floorward in one hand, he reached in his coat pocket and palmed out a bright brass object, a cartridge case. "Your heel dog, suh, owns a shiny new cannon, a center-fire Colt's .45." He nodded toward the commode top, where Keno Paul's pistol lay. "The shells it takes are quite distinctive. They have this tiny central depression in the priming cap made to receive a firing pin. A shell like this one."

Keno Paul flicked his tongue over his lips; he jerked a fleeting look at Renard, whose face was still calm. "Interesting," said Renard. "Where did you find it?"

"Well, now, it stands to reason whoever shot Muley from that alley mouth would clear out fast. He would head back down the alley and he would be running hard. Does that make sense?"

Renard didn't reply.

"So that's where I looked for running-hard track this morning. I found it all right, though it petered out where our man slowed down and then held to the hard packed ground back of the buildings. About the time he did, though, he decided to shuck this spent shell, and that's where I found it. He was getting rid of evidence, he thought, but handed me a nice piece of it instead. Not that it would mean much, but for your man's center-fire weapon being the only one in Peaceville, a matter we shall duly confirm."

A hint of squeezed desperation had touched Keno Paul's face, but Renard only looked blandly bored. "As I said—interesting. But hardly the sort of evidence that will stand up in a court of law."

"Won't it, though?" Doc said just as blandly. "Think about it, Jess. Any jury that sits on the case will be made up of local people—merchants, settlers, and the like—who are anxious to see you and other crooked operators sent packing. I would say they'll be wide open and receptive to any kind of evidence, especially—" he played the trump card now "—since Muley Foran died an hour ago."

Keno Paul whirled suddenly and snatched the .45 off the commode, cocking and leveling it all in one motion. "There won't be no evidence," he said huskily. "I'll take that shell, hide hunter."

"You damned fool!" Renard rasped. "It's a bluff, they can't *prove*—"

"It's my neck, not yours." A sheen of sweat glazed Keno Paul's face; his jaw shook. "Mine that'll get stretched, anyways. Give me that damn shell, or—"

Rhiannon was motionless, his rifle pointed down. Then he shrugged. "Just as you say, friend. It is not so important to us anyway. You have already been thrown to the wolves."

"What? What do you mean by that?"

"Ask Renard. He sold you out."

Keno Paul's widening eyes flicked to Renard's face. In that instant Rhiannon lashed up one-handed with his Sharps, the muzzle smacking the dealer's gunhand upward. His reflexive jerk of the trigger sent his shot thundering into the ceiling. Rhiannon's great bulk came hard into him now, pinning him against the commode. Rhiannon wrested the pistol away and then stepped back.

"You double-damned idiot," Renard whispered. "They had no real proof, and we could've got you a change of venue." He looked bitterly at Doc and Rhiannon. "We'll still do it. By God, we'll see!"

"Do that," Doc said mildly. "We can take what just happened to any other damned court, Jess. Your boy here has tipped your hand very nicely. Whatever happens now, you're through in Peaceville.

Rhiannon motioned toward the door. "I would reckon that you two know where the jail is." He grinned. "Funny thing is, *I* don't."

"You'll learn," said Doc. "You've learned a thing or two already—like how to keep your bristles in place. Or have you?"

Rhiannon nodded wryly. "I'm getting there, Doc. I have been a wild boar of the prairie for too long, I reckon."

At the general merchandise store a half an hour later, Doc told the two O'Herlihys all about Rhiannon's accomplishment with as many expansive flourishes as he could throw in, not trusting Ox Rhiannon to handle the tale of his own regeneration without cutting himself on the rough edges. Molly listened wide-eyed, but smiling a little, as if she'd figured on it all along, while Regis nodded and scowled and chewed on the stem of his pipe.

When Doc had finished, O'Herlihy stuck out his hand to Ox, saying gruffly, "Lad, I'd invite ye to dinner, but all we're having is crow, with humble pie for dessert."

WESTWARD THEY RODE

Doc chuckled, noting the exchange of self-conscious looks between Ox Rhiannon and Molly. "It's a new day for Peaceville, Regis."

"Aye, Mordaunt. A good one for all."

Doc took the storekeeper's arm and propelled him toward the door. "What do you say we start it off with a drink?"

NO-FIGHTS

He found the old woman's body where it had fallen by the travois trail of crushed grasses. She looked like a dirty bundle of rags among the bent grass stems. The thin lids were drawn shut over her eyes as if she had gone to sleep—and perhaps such was the case—but from this sleep there would be no waking.

No-Fights parted the grasses and bent, gently lifting her in his arms. He carried her back toward the brow of the hill where two silent women waited, daughter and granddaughter of the dead one. No-Fights stepped slowly, hating the twisted lame foot that held him to a painful hobble.

This was a bad place and a bad time of day to delay the march, for the stop had caught them on high and open ground.

Though it was late August and the northern prairie simmered under the ripening heat of full summer and the hills were full of chokecherries and wild plum and fat jackrabbits, the people of the Lakotas had seldom known a more bitter time.

The beginning of this summer had seen the annihilation of Long Hair Custer and his troops. On the western bank of the river of Greasy Grass, known to the whites as Little Big Horn, Sioux, Cheyenne, and Arapaho had gathered twelve thousand strong for the great battle. Afterward they had split up again, and the broken bands had spent an uneasy summer following the buffalo herds, drying meat against the time they would be driven back to the reservations and a starvation diet. Now the country was swarming with patrols of grim-eyed soldiers. Drum telegraph and smoke signal kept the Indians informed that the Gray Fox, General Crook, was pressing the relentless hunt.

Ah! How they had exulted that night at the wild victory dance on Lodge Grass Creek in the shadow of the Big Horn Mountains. And how quickly victory had turned to ashes. Already the Cheyenne leader, Yellow Hand, was dead, slain by the white scout Cody in a bitter duel at Warbonnet Creek. Yellow Hand's people were back on the reservation. And what of the buffalo, source of the sustenance, the clothing, the shelter that *Wakun Tanta* had provided for his children? What of those endless swarms of bison that had blackened the hills only fifteen years ago? The southern herd was gone. Now, encouraged by an angry government, the hide hunters were making deep inroads into the northern herd. From victory had come defeat; the crushing of Long Hair, their most treacherous and hated enemy, had marked the end of something, and they all knew it.

No, this was no time for a halt to be forced on a lone Lakota and the two women in his care. But No-Fights had searched his heart and found he had no choice. Probably the old one had quietly rolled off the travois on which she rode behind the others and their horses, feeling that her time had come and hoping they would not note her absence till they were far from here. But less than a quarter of a mile on, Pretty Shield had taken notice. Halting the horses, No-Fights had gone back to look. What else could he do? He knew how his wife had loved her grandmother. It was she who had pain ed Pretty Shield's body for her puberty ritual; it was she who had served as intermediary, trotting patiently back and forth between their lodges, during the long, elaborate period of their courtship. He too had been fond of the old woman.

Unspeaking, he laid the light, shrunken corpse at the feet of the two women. No-Fights' mother-in-law began to wail on her knees. He ignored her, but not from disrespect; he was not permitted to speak to her or even look at her directly.

He spoke to his wife, "We cannot stop long. There will be no four days of mourning, not even one day. You will dress her and I will make a platform."

There was no timber close by, but he could fashion a crude burial scaffold of brush. No-Fig' ts started downhill toward a dense clot of thickets. Then his slight, slender body froze in midstep as he stared below the dropping sun at a group of horsemen coming down a tawny slope.

Soldiers. Even from here he could recognize their uniforms. There were only four blue-shirted men riding in a sloppy bunch, which seemed strange, but all that was important at the moment was his own stupidity at calling the halt on a hilltop where they were clearly visible against the sky. And that they had been seen there could be no doubt, for the soldiers were coming this way in an un' urried beeline.

No-Fights stood where he was, unmoving except for

WESTWARD THEY RODE

gently rubbing his palm along one smoke-tanned legging. These men were coming from the direction of Fort Abraham Lincoln to the south, and this would surely be no truce encounter, not with that fort's late commander and two hundred and twenty of their comrades less than two moons in their graves.

No-Fights thought of the bow and arrows under the hide cover on the travois. No, these were no medicine against four *wasicun* with guns. He could have cursed with the white man's obscenities he had learned at mission school, thinking of old Crooked Horn and his two hulking sons riding off with all three rifles this morning.

All he could do was stand and wait and plan how best to dissemble. He had learned of ways to behave around white men. In such a situation as this, a certain affected deference could tip a fine balance between life and death. Buffalo Calf Woman, his mother-in-law, had ceased her wailing, for the women too, attracted by his stance, had seen the soldiers.

In a short time the riders were coming up the hill. The man in the lead halted briefly, looking down at him.

"Hullo," this one said crisply. He was as lean as a whiplash, with eyes like chilled steel. No-Fights, arms hanging loose at his sides, let an empty, wondering smile break across his face.

The man reined on past him, the other three following. The second, a black-bearded giant, scowled at No-Fights as he swung by, fingering the Springfield on his pommel in a longing manner. After him came a sallow, ugly youth whose hair, under a battered campaign hat, was so pale it looked white. He led the fourth man's horse. This *wasicun* was slumped on his horse's withers.

173

Blood soaked the faded blue shirt over his stocky trunk. He was almost unconscious; his baby face under its bristly yellow hair was screwed up like a dried fruit.

No-Fights limped slowly up the hill, warily watching the four men dismount by the lead travois. The leader's steel eyes seemed to miss nothing. Black Beard stepped to the ground, rubbing his rump and damning McClellan saddles until his heavy-lidded glance touched Pretty Shield. He whistled; he smiled hugely.

"Hey." He looked at No-Fights. "Your squaw, huh, John? How much she worth you?"

"Leave them alone, you bloody idiot," the steel-eyed man said. "We'll need their help for Fritz and antagonizing them won't get it."

Black Beard massaged his rump with both hands and shelved out his shaggy chin at No-Fights, winking. "Hey, how much you want squaw? Money, huh? How much she worth you, John?"

No-Fights grinned foolishly. His jaws were starting to ache. "No savvy."

"Rawlings. Let them alone, I said."

Black Beard turned ponderously, dropping his slab-like hands. "Ain't nobody made you gen'ril that I know of, Robertson."

The steel-eyed one slowly opened the flap of his pistol holster. "Think I might rank you when all's said. Care to lay a small wager?"

Rawlings tugged his beard; he grunted. "Naw. I seen you use a hogleg. That ain't no bet I'd last to pay."

"Well then, you're a wise gorilla, after all," Robertson murmured. His eye lighted on the withered form in the grass. "I say, what's that? Oh, I see. Old woman's dead. Must have stopped to bury her or whatever they do."

No-Fights carefully reconnoitered the situation. It was not a good one. Something was not quite right about these four men. But for the uniforms they might have been gold hunters; there was nothing of the white soldier's well-drilled discipline in their relationship to each other or in their manners. This one, the leader, spoke strangely. He must be one of those not born of the Americans. There were many such among the soldiers, some of them exiles and outlaws from their own lands, it was said.

The steel gaze swung on him. "All right, my friend. We don't wish you or yours any harm. Just a bit of rum luck and we need your help. You red fellows know about healing herbs and the like, or so I've heard."

No-Fights smiled vapidly, and Robertson frowned. "H'm. Let's see. Ah, man heap sick. You help? You got medicine—heal up all well—eh?" Impatience flickered in his gray, metal-colored eyes.

There were times, No-Fights knew, when it was adroit not to play too ignorant. By carefully broken English and signs he conveyed to Robertson that Buffalo Calf Woman would look at the wounded soldier, but that it would be well to make camp down below where there was good water.

"Good idea," Robertson nodded. "Too open up here. Bad place. All right, lend a hand, you fellows. Rawlings, we'll lay Fritz on this horse drag; he's about done up. Kamas," this to the sallow youth, "keep an eye on these people."

With the hurt soldier on one travois and the dead grandmother on the other, they moved down the northeast flank of the long slope into its lengthening shadow. The dipping eye of the sun made the limitless waves of grass a sea of fluid gold. At the bottom of the hill, where the stream was, they set up bivouac. Robertson's crisp orders to his companions made the work go quickly. Four of the lodge poles formed the two travois; the remaining poles had been lashed to one travois, the buffalo hide cover to the other, with the household articles tied across these or to the women's saddles. Now the travois were quickly dismantled, the sixteen poles arranged in a rough cone. No-Fights grunted directions so that the poles on the windward side would be the short ones, and he made sure the two poles controlling the smoke flaps were properly set. The cover, made of eleven sewn hides, was not in place before Buffalo Calf Woman was digging the rectangular fireplace in the center of the floor.

Pretty Shield brought in the furniture: willow-stick backrests, willow-reed mattresses and tule mats, and the rawhide parfleches and deerhide bags used for storage. She knelt to arrange these things. She was wearing, besides her high moccasins, only a scanty camp dress of soft-beaten doehide, sleeveless and short-skirted. Rawlings stopped tugging at the buffalo hide cover to peer at the glossy brown knees, round and dimpling, as she knelt. No-Fights' aching jaw tightened more as he began to hate.

But he kept his direct gaze on his work. For some reason these white soldiers seemed tractably disposed, and he did not want to arouse them. His father-in-law, Crooked Horn, had ridden out with his two sons early this morning to find fresh meat. There were a few buffalo ranging toward the east, and last night, when striking camp, they had seen a distant herd of pronghorn in the same area. The rest of Crooked Horn's little family, under No-Fights' protection, had kept on the move.

When would Crooked Horn and his sons return? No-Fights was worried that they would frolic into camp with their usual hard-riding impetuosity, straight into the guns of the white men. That would be a shame, since the white men were ignorant of their existence and could easily be taken by surprise. As it was, there would be shooting that would endanger the women. He hoped that the whites would depart before Crooked Horn's return, for it appeared likely that the four intended them no harm for the present and might even let them go their way if Buffalo Calf Woman gave the hurt one good care.

Simply thinking of Crooked Horn, the old devil, put a sour taste in No-Fights' mouth. Neither Pretty Shield's father nor her brothers made any secret of their contempt for their slight, crippled brother-in-law. Sioux custom had dictated that he become a member of his bride's family, this normally being a reciprocal and pleasant arrangement, but he had brought too few horses to Crooked Horn's hearth, he was a poor hunter who had not yet killed enough buffalo to make even a small tipi for himself and his wife and, as a warrior, he had proven virtually useless. All this being so, the affection and welcome he had a right to expect as a new son and lodge brother was not forthcoming. Also, Pretty Shield had been a popular girl who had walked with many a young man in his blanket. Good warriors and fine horse catchers, their courting gifts of mounts had added impressively to Crooked Horn's small herd. The family could neither understand nor forgive Pretty Shield's miserable choice of a husband.

That No-Fights' quiet tastes ran to crafts and arts and deep thinking rather than to more vigorous pursuits had in no way helped matters. The Sioux did not discourage arts or artisans; indeed, a youth was generously trained in whatever direction his talents and interests pointed. But Crooked Horn and his boys took a dim view of anything not smacking of war or the hunt, calling any man who shunned them a "half-woman." By way of extenuation, the old man liked to catalogue white abuses at obsessive length, the broken treaties and dwindling game herds and assorted atrocities—such as Long Hair's massacre of Black Kettle and his Cheyennes on the Washita eight grasses ago—but the fact was that Crooked Horn was a troublemaker. "Too much head, too little heart, is no good," he would say pointedly, obviously referring to his sorry son-in-law. He liked to boast of his own part in the Spirit Lake massacre in Minnesota fourteen grasses back to illustrate his point. As a chief of the Santee Sioux, Crooked Horn had helped instigate the killing of hundreds of white settlers. He played down the sequel, which was that he had escaped being hanged only because the White Grandfather called Lincoln had interceded at the last minute with pardons for all but thirty-eight of the Indian ringleaders.

Despite Crooked Horn's windy bragging, everybody guessed that his close call had been a sobering influence, for he had moved his family to the Great Plains and joined the Teton Sioux, No-Fights' people. However he had not adjusted well to the ways of his western cousins; his obstreperous and quarrelsome nature had upset the tenor of their lives. First he had been warned by the warriors' society. Next publicly ridiculed by the women. Finally his tipi had been torn down in public view, and in a raging huff, Crooked Horn had taken his family and goods and departed. Ostracization would have been the next step anyway.

No-Fights had been sorry to lose friends he had known all his life, sorry to abandon the relative safety and comforts of village life, but he would have been sorrier to lose Pretty Shield. He had accompanied his wife's family, much to Crooked Horn's disgust. A shame, the latter often declared loudly for his daughter's ears, since divorce was a simple matter of public declaration; but Pretty Shield pretended never to hear.

While the men scoured up firewood and tended the horses, Buffalo Calf Woman treated the injured soldier's wound with powdered sage and medicinal herbs and made a wrapping of the shed wool of a buffalo bull. She did a good job of it, No-Fights noted approvingly. They must avoid offending these *wasicun* in any way.

The sun had heeled deep into the west, and No-Fights indicated his wish to erect a burial scaffold before darkness came. He would need his hatchet. Robertson was agreeable, but told the youth named Kamas to go along with a rifle.

No-Fights found a grove of cottonwood downstream and cut a number of saplings which he lashed together into a lofty platform. With the help of the women, while the white men looked on, he lifted the grandmother's tightly wrapped body atop it. Pretty Shield hacked her hair off short and Buffalo Calf Woman gashed her legs and wailed some more. Rawlings growled that if she did not shut up he would slit her tongue, and Robertson passed the suggestion along more politely but just as definitely.

"It is no good making the white ones mad," No-Fights

pointed out to his wife. "Soon, if we are lucky, they will be gone."

Pretty Shield was in a pet. "I do not like how the one with hair on his face looks at me. Why do you not kill him? Why do you smile at these white men and stutter in their stupid tongue? Has your heart turned to water?"

The words had a bitter ring to his ears. "*Henala*," he muttered, eying her in mild astonishment. He was used to this kind of talk from her family, but how could Pretty Shield think such a thing of him? He put the question to her.

"I do not know," she said sullenly. "If you are not scratching the earth like a dog for these men, still you *act* the part and that is bad enough. If the hairy face touches me, I will kill him."

To a Sioux woman nothing was more sacred than her virginity prior to marriage and her wifely honor afterward. The trouble was, No-Fights knew worriedly, few white men believed it. But beyond this, he was stunned by her confessed doubt of him. Perhaps her father had succeeded in planting a doubt which had been hidden till now. He supposed, if it came to that, he was afraid of what the whites would do; but mostly his fear was on her account. Playing the fool was no part of real courage that he could see.

Rawlings' hot black eyes followed Pretty Shield as she went to get water. When she returned, the black-bearded one made a grab for her and was rewarded by a quick slash of her small knife even as she evaded his reach. Rawlings howled and clutched his nicked wrist. He would, he promised, kill the bitch, and suited action to words by pulling his pistol.

The crisp sound of a gun being cocked halted the big man's movements.

Robertson was sitting by the smoke flaps, his pistol carelessly trained on Rawlings. Negligently he removed his pipe from his mouth. "I say, Rawlings, you're being an ass, you know. Pity if I had to kill you over such a trifle."

Rawlings swung, half-crouching; his eyes were red in the firelight. "But nice for you, huh? If Fritz cashes it, you and Kamas could split the gold two——"

"Shut up, you ruddy fool." Robertson's gaze bored against No-Fights and the two women, then swung back to the big man. "That's enough."

"Too bad," Rawlings said. "Deserting was your idea, and if killing them two prospectors was mine, you was pretty quick to fall in with the idea."

Robertson gave a resigned sigh and shook his head, as if the damage were done and there was no point in fussing. He holstered his gun and looked on wearily as Rawlings tore open his saddlebag to dig out a bottle of *mui waken*, the white man's holy water which made the world look better and often led to visions. No-Fights noticed the heavy thud the bag made when Rawlings dropped it again.

As few of the communal-living Sioux did, No-Fights had a firm understanding of the whites' feeling for personal wealth. His mission-school training was responsible, but with his reflective mind, understanding had brought contempt, not sympathy. He knew, as did all the Sioux, that it was Long Hair's finding gold when he had visited the Black Hills two years ago to make a treaty with the conclave of chiefs (and which he had amusedly broken by spreading word of the strike so that the treaty lands were soon overrun with white gold hunters) that had led to their current trouble.

The two women prepared a stew of dried meat and wild turnips. It was a desire to relieve the monotony of this diet that had sent Crooked Horn and his sons far afield for meat. While the copper pot bubbled, Rawlings sat cross-legged and pulled at his *mui waken*. Finally, his eyes glazed with its holy effect, he produced a rawhide sack from his saddle and spilled some of the sparkling dust it contained into his palm. His gaze grew faraway as he examined it by the firelight.

This was gold; there were more such little sacks in the saddlebag, and No-Fights was beginning to understand.

Much of what had been a puzzle about these men became ever more clear during the course of the meal. From random fragments of Rawlings' boisterous, spirits-inspired talk, No-Fights learned that the four of them, each for his own reasons, had deserted the garrison at Fort Abraham Lincoln. They had decided to throw in together and head for Canada, where Robertson's uncle owned a ranch. Early today they had come on the camp of two ancient prospectors who, seeing their uniforms, had boasted too readily and trustingly of their good fortune. After availing themselves of the prospectors' hospitality, the four deserters had murdered the prospectors and split up the gold on the spot. One of the pair had managed to put a bullet into Fritz before he was killed.

To No-Fights, his own situation, as well as that of the women, was suddenly, brutally clear. There was no way of telling whether the one called Robertson had ever really intended letting them go unharmed. But Rawlings' loud betrayal of the two murders had made certain that these white deserters could not afford to let the three of them live to tell what they knew to the soldiers who would finally overtake them and return them to the reservation. Their lives, No-Fights guessed, would be safe only while the white men needed Buffalo Calf Woman to treat the wounded one.

Twice, as the evening wore on, Rawlings restored the gold to the sack, only to return to it and sift it through his fingers in a distant trance.

No-Fights sat in his blanket, his thoughts black and bitter. He was tough and wiry, but small, and his physical strength was not great. He flexed his bad leg, the lifelong legacy of a childhood fall. Yet he would have seized any chance at all to overcome one of these men, except that the remaining two would effect his own death that much sooner.

He would stand no chance against all three at once, that was certain. He measured the three through half-lidded eyes, appraising their strengths and weaknesses. Presently, by grunts and signs, he told Robertson that there was insufficient wood to keep the fire alive much longer; he would fetch more. Robertson assented and, as No-Fights had hoped, told Kamas to accompany him.

Taking the hatchet, the young Sioux headed out along the creek which glittered in the moonlight. Kamas followed him at a casual but cautious distance, rifle in hand. No-Fights hacked an armload of brush while watching Kamas from the tail of his eye. His palm itched with the impulse to throw the hatchet at the sallow one in a single, swift movement. As a boy he had practiced much with the throwing ax. But he let caution flag down the temptation.

No-Fights made two trips for wood, and on the second

he quietly jammed the hatchet deep in the thick grass where the sloping stream bank was veiled by the deep shadows of fringing brush. How this would help he could only conjecture, but at least he had a hidden weapon.

As he had hoped, the slow-witted Kamas missed the surreptitious action and forgot to ask for the hatchet when they returned to the lodge. A further stroke of luck was that Robertson and Rawlings were arguing and took bare notice of their return. These two, but especially Robertson, would be harder to trick.

"We oughta move on now," Rawlings was grumbling. "Cover all the ground we can while it's dark."

"No," Robertson said crisply. "I'll desert an army any day, but not a hurt comrade. We'll not leave this spot until Fritz can ride."

"Hell, he ain't gonna live out the night. Look at him."

The yellow-haired one's condition was worsening, there could be no doubt. His ruddy color had faded to a pasty gray; fever and delirium were on him. He was bundled in blankets, yet was wracked by violent chills.

"Perhaps not," Robertson agreed. "But live or die, we'll wait him out—unless you care to go on alone? We've divided up the gold."

"Naw." The black-beard shook his head vigorously. "Not with them wild Injuns that got Custer running all over the country."

"Then shut up and listen. We'll split the night into three watches, two hours apiece. Which will you take?"

"We don't need to watch *him*," Rawlings protested, waving a contemptuous hand at No-Fights. "That runty siwash couldn't stomp his own nits and he ain't got the brains God gives gophers."

No-Fights beamed his vapid appreciation of the white man's notice.

Robertson gave the Sioux a long, keen appraisal. "H'm. Perhaps so. But what about that young she-devil with the knife? Which watch, boys?"

Kamas volunteered for the first, and Rawlings, scowling, said he'd take the second. Robertson yawned and stretched out on his blankets. "Jolly good. Me for the dawn one, then. And see here, old chap, keep your paws off that girl. Confine your wooing to Morpheus, understand?"

Rawlings growled unintelligibly and rolled into his blankets. No-Fights eased himself onto his side, wondering about this Robertson's strange loyalty to a helpless companion when he could casually murder other white men for their gold. There was only one aspect of the *wasicun* in which the young Sioux held full confidence: their greed.

He tried to catch Pretty Shield's eye for a glance of understanding and reassurance, but she refused to look at him. He felt vaguely pained in his chest. She wanted her man to play the man she had always believed him to be, whatever others might think. But he had to do this thing his way. The differences that separated him from his fellows went deeper than physical; they embraced mind and heart. He cared little what the others thought, but he wanted Pretty Shield to understand.

As the other occupants of the lodge drifted into sleep, he stayed awake and alert. Kamas sat by the fire, knees drawn up, the rifle propped between them. No-Fights lay on his side facing the fire, his blanket tucked cowl-like about his head so that he could feign sleep while peering out between the folds. He watched Kamas sink into a light doze time after time, always snapping himself erect again. Finally his head tilted solidly onto his knees, and he slept.

No-Fights did not twitch a muscle. What to do now? He could not secure any of their guns without waking them. Perhaps he could steal outside and get the hatchet, but suppose he succeeded in killing one, only to wake the others?

He stirred the folds wider, letting his eyes move. Rawlings' gold-filled saddlebag lay perhaps the length of his leg away. No-Fights smiled.

He spent the space of many heartbeats inching close to the bag and securing one of the heavy rawhide pokes inside it. Painstakingly, then, he raised himself on an elbow and gently tossed the gold sack across the lodge, holding his breath as it thudded softly between the skin wall and Robertson's blanket-wrapped form. The man sighed and stirred but slept on.

No-Fights maneuvered back to his former position, watching and waiting. At last Kamas jerked awake and looked about with furtive guilt. Hastily he consulted an old watch, then went to shake Rawlings awake for his watch, afterward turning in. Kamas snored off at once.

Rawlings squatted by the fire, occasionally pulling moodily at his half-empty bottle, restlessly wrapping and unwrapping the stained bandanna that covered the little cut on his arm. He eyed Pretty Shield's recumbent form with a burning hunger. No-Fights' muscles tightened into aching knots.

Finally, as he had hoped, Rawlings rose and tramped heavily over to his saddlebag. He carried it back to the fire, sat down and fumbled the bag open. Almost at once came his feral curse. He scrambled about the floor on his hands and knees, looking wildly. Then his glance of dawning suspicion found Kamas. Shouting incoherently, he dragged the sallow youth out of his blanket, slapping him with vicious, open-handed blows.

"Where is it, damn you, maybe you thought I never counted my pokes! Where is it, damn you—"

Robertson, sitting upright, gave a curt order. Rawlings flung Kamas to the ground and stood spraddle-legged, looming over the other man in the firelight, his massive fists closing and unclosing.

"Don't be a fool," Robertson snapped. "Kamas wouldn't—"

"He was on watch, wa'n't he?" Rawlings' huge shoulders stiffened then; his arm swung up. "There it is, right beside you!"

Robertson looked blankly down. The bulging gold sack lay only a foot from his elbow.

"That's it, the two of you," Rawlings bellowed. "You are in this together, fixing to cross me up."

"You drunken—" Robertson began, but his words were drowned in the flat roar of Rawlings' pistol.

Caught sitting, Robertson had time for one abortive movement before the slug smashed the bridge of his nose.

No-Fights was already on his feet. But his head was cool in the confusion; he tried neither to fight nor to run on his bad leg. He made a strong, lunging dive that carried him through the smoke flaps into the night.

Lighting on his side, he let his momentum take him on a short distance, rolling, before he scrambled to his feet. He broke through the brush and tumbled down the shadowy stream bank, skidding on his belly close to the water. His outflung hand groped for, and was rewarded by, the smooth familiar grip on the hatchet.

Rawlings was yelling that they had been tricked. "Watch them women!" he roared.

Hugging the bank with his belly and face, No-Fights heard the thud of heavy feet coming from the lodge. Rawlings was cursing fretfully as he circled the lodge. Then he started along the top of the stream bank, poking at the brush, quite careless and noisy because he thought No-Fights was unarmed.

Cautiously the Sioux raised himself to his knees. The soldier's bull head and shoulders topped the brush. He was skylined at a distance of about the length of three tall men as he stopped, beating a thicket with his pistol.

No-Fights whipped his arm back and forward. The hatchet blade caught a fitful moonbeam, turning over once in its short flight.

Rawlings' eye caught the flash of steel or perhaps the motion of No-Fights' arm. The startled grunt that erupted from his chest ended in a gurgling sigh. He toppled with a crash into the brush and rolled down through it to the water's edge.

No-Fights crawled to the body and pried the thick fingers away from the pistol grip. From the lodge, Kamas was querulously calling Rawlings by name.

No-Fight had never held a weapon he had taken in battle; he felt the fierce pride of his birthright leap high in his breast. He wanted to run out and confront the last white man. But always his cool head was master; he, who had scarcely held a gun in all his life, would have little chance thus.

So he loped noiselessly up the bank and waited behind the dark brush until Kamas showed himself against the firelight in the tipi entrance. Then No-Fights took careful aim. . . .

During the night, the one called Fritz died quietly in his sleep. No-Fights thought about it awhile before deciding to bury the white men after their own fashion, rather than letting the bodies achieve a properly advanced state of decomposition before ground burial, as was customary with the Sioux. No-Fights, who took a jaundiced view of most customs, cared little one way or another; he merely wanted to test Pretty Shield. He brusquely told her to start digging and she, with an adoring glance, meekly knelt and attacked the prairie sod with a bone tool.

While they were so engaged, No-Fights dozing in the shade, Pretty Shield sweating beneath the sun, her mother hunting for wild turnips nearby, Crooked Horn and his two boys returned, riding up with exuberant whoops. Hunting had been good; the packhorse carried the hides of two butchered pronghorns, the skins hanging down on either side with the choice cuts folded inside and the big, marrow-sweet bones tied on top.

The three halted, looking from their busy daughter and sister to the three blanket-wrapped bodies, from the glowering Kamas sitting propped against a lodge pole with his wounded leg stretched out, to their somnolent son-in-law who did not rise, only the movement of his eyes offering sleepy acknowledgement of their return.

Bad-Heart Bull, the older son and born clown, tried to jest away the incredible sight. "Ho! Look at the soldiers our little sister has slain while her husband slept," he laughed, but Crooked Horn cut him off with a glance. He motioned his wife over and soon had the story.

To No-Fights he said, "Why is this one alive? All soldiers are our enemies."

No-Fights stirred his shoulders against the earth. "I did not want to kill him," he explained idly.

"Why?" demanded White-Man-Running, the belligerent younger son. "Did your heart turn to water?"

No-Fights watched him steadily. "I do not like to kill. There was no need."

"What," asked Crooked Horn, "will you do with him?" There might have been the merest note of respect in his tone.

"Let him go without horse or gun. He is hurt. If the prairie does not kill him, the soldiers will find him and shoot him. He ran away from their army."

Crooked Horn appeared pleased by the idea, but the sons continued to strut and taunt, ridiculing No-Fights in the old manner after he admitted that he had not counted coup on even one of his enemies, had not risked his life to strike one without inflicting injury.

It was Buffalo Calf Woman who finally interceded, fiercely castigating her sons. "Fools! You think there is no way to fight but with your muscles, your great mouths, your stupid coup-counting. I tell you, my son-in-law has fought with his head, his good brains, and so we are alive. Where would we be if one of you, and not he, had been here? I will tell you. Dead, all dead!"

No-Fights yawned ostentatiously and shut his eyes. He would have liked to show Buffalo Calf Woman his gratitude by even a fleeting glance, but not to wholly ignore her would be very bad form. Even a different one could observe some traditions comfortably.

THEY WALKED TALL

"Walk with your head up," my Pa used to say. "Walk tall. Never look down. Good sense to be afraid only so long as a man don't show it. Man who don't look down never backs down."

Pa was built to see other men from that perspective. In a country of big men he stood bigger than most. He was six-four in his sock feet, broad as a beam and hickory-hard. Not that he misused his size, not by his own standards. He was a pioneer, a builder, not a destroyer. Most always his eyes had the look of far blue horizons. And there were other times, warning times, when they flashed small lightnings.

Pa had been a captain of cavalry in the Army of Northern Virginia. "Then damn Rec'nstructers and carpetbag politicos wouldn't let a Southern man hold up his head on his native ground," he used to growl. "Man's got to keep a tight fist around his pride or he's nothing." He'd settled into Wyoming as the first flush of gold seekers were drifting out and the cow barons were on the rise.

It was natural that Pa go into cattle, building his Sickle spread from a shoestring. He built sturdy, built to last. He worked from sunup till dusk, bossing his three-man crew. When he married my Ma he threw up a tight stone house under the Absaroka peaks, cool in summer and warm in winter. It fitted the country like a hand in a glove; it was a good place, a good life. Pa didn't overset his sights, but he built with an eye to permanence. He ran his small herd on open range and forced respect even from Hugh Buckhorn.

Old Buckhorn owned the huge Chainlink outfit which sprawled over all the eastern half of our valley except for the mountain-backed pocket where our Sickle was nested. This Buckhorn was an old-time settler who'd grown to a purse-proud son. While Pa stablized his holdings, Buckhorn got the fever of expansion. He claimed up to and around our Sickle proper, moseying over our open range some, but not over the patented line, you can bet. Buckhorn was mean and tough. Pa was only tough, but that was enough.

The other little ranchers kept over on the west side of the valley; they were careful about that, except at roundup time.

Funny thing how Pa's mettle was never really tried until this nester man come, first of his kind in the valley. Joe Lynch was a hardscrabble sort who set out to crop his quarter section astride Tie Creek, a horseshoe stream which enclosed Sickle. It was the unspoken boundary betwixt us and Buckhorn, as far as open range went. This Lynch took over an old Chainlink line shack long-time abandoned by the outfit and moved in with his tired drudge of a wife and their tow-headed brood of five. Joe Lynch was a worker. He fixed up the shack and made most of his homestead improvements inside of a couple weeks.

Pa glowered and muttered some, but generally he stood by the law. Anyway—and he sounded positive—

WESTWARD THEY RODE

this wasn't farm country. Few nesters might come and stick a year or so till the land licked 'em and move on, leaving the valley flats to grass and cattle as the Lord meant them to be.

I make it the real trouble came when Joe Lynch brought in barbed wire, what the old, free-ranging cowmen hated most—and maybe feared—for it was the end of a time.

I was twelve, that early summer of '88. It comes back like yesterday how on a certain sunny morning I came in for breakfast from doing the first chores. Ours was a warm little household, and I smelled out right off that something wasn't right.

Here was the old man sitting and putting away corn bread, bacon and coffee with his ordinary appetite, and Ma, as usual, bustling back and forth between stove and table. Only the stubborn blue of Pa's eyes was flicking little lightnings, and Ma's back had a stiff angry set and her round, strong face was flushed with more than oven heat. I edged over to the woodbox and eased down my armload of wood, so as not to bust up all this quiet, and took my place across from Pa.

The old man cleaned up his plate and lighted his pipe. I knowed he was waiting on me, so I ate fast, so fast that Ma scolded, "Tim, for heaven's sake."

Soon's I'd gulped the last mouthful, Pa said quietly, "Boy, you leave the rest of them chores. You ride with me today."

Ma swung around from the stove, quick and sharp. "Jud Tasker, you'll not take the boy with you. It's bad enough having this un-Christian thing in your head without it taking in him."

Pa acted like he didn't hear. That was his way. He just

went ahead and never wasted a breath. "You know why, Timmy, eh?"

"We taking the crew?"

In those days range gossip was a wildfire kind of thing —kids, parents, the old ones—they all knew when something was up. I expect I sounded eager as any cub, because Pa smiled a little. "No, boy. This here's between me and Joe Lynch."

The grin faded as he looked at Ma, like he wanted to make her understand. "Martha, now I told the boy never to back water. Words got an empty sound without a body takes to their meaning."

Ma wouldn't look at him.

He sighed and shoved back his chair and walked to the east wall. He took down the Spencer .54 repeater carbine he had taken off a dead Yankee trooper twenty-four years ago. It had been converted to take metal-jacketed cartridges. He broke out a fresh box of shells and loaded her up. I had seen him do as much aplenty, loading for varmint, but this bright morning those smooth metal noises made my scalp prickle.

Pa lifted off his hat from a wall peg and didn't look back when he walked out, me close on his heels. We saddled up down at the corral, Pa cinching his rig on his rangy lineback dun and waiting while I threw a hull across the whey-bellied old mare.

We cut west over the rolling, grass-grown flats to Tie Creek. I kept off behind the old man where I could see only the gnarled-oak set of his big back and one hard edge of black-bearded jaw. I was some squirrelly, I tell you, but also fair to split for wanting to see Pa give that damn' nester what for.

Pa only said one thing the whole ride, "You mark your

Ma, boy. Got a heart big as all outdoors. Just don't understand these things. Mostly a woman don't. Ain't to say your Ma don't know aplenty in her own right, you mind me?"

I minded, all right, but there wasn't a lot of sense to it. It doesn't mean much at twelve that a man's got his ways, a woman hers. What sense I made was that Pa meant there would be no disrespect to Ma on this account. If I showed any, his broad leather belt would come off fast. I cleared my throat and said, "Yes, sir," making it as respectful as I knew how.

In an hour we came in sight of Tie Creek winding between its low banks like a sparkling snake. Pa turned upstream toward Lynch's homestead. We'd gone maybe a half mile when we came on this line of new peeled posts lined by three tight strands, barbed and shiny. It was kind of a wall, and I felt Pa's temper crackle inside my own head. He rode up to one post and leaned from his saddle and grabbed it. He gave a hard tug, but it was ground-braced, solid against his big muscles. He said something under his breath, heeled the lineback around and headed up the line of posts at a fast trot.

We came up on a grassy knoll and saw the nester's wagon pulled up below. The bed was piled high with fresh-cut cedar posts; a couple rolls of new wire were under the seat. This Joe Lynch was on the ground working with wire stretchers and pliers, putting all his stringy muscle into pulling that damn' wire drum tight. He was too intent to see us as we came on down the slope.

Pa's voice froze the nester as he bent over to fetch up a staple from the keg by his feet. He came up slow, trying to straighten his shoulders. They were thin and work-stooped. He wiped his hands on his pants.

"Morning, Mr. Tasker," Lynch said. I don't know that he was so scared, but he sounded on a caution for sure.

Pa never wasted time. He didn't now. He looked at the posts, nodding as if to himself. "These here'll have to come down. When it turns cold, my cattle'll drift with the winds and pile against 'em. First'll be cut to ribbons, rest'll pile three, four deep, freeze that way."

Pa was making reference to a couple years past when the Great Blizzard of '86 hit the high plains. That had been no ordinary time; even I knew as much. The amount of wire around Joe Lynch's little homestead might catch a few far-drifting beeves, no more.

Lynch, he thumb-nudged the slouch hat back on his lean towhead, being uncertain about it all. "Well, that could be so, Mr. Tasker. Me and mine are fresh out of Ohio, you know."

Pa swelled a little. "I reckon. No cattle of mine been grazing this way, no call for all this. Man, are you meaning to wave a red flag under my nose?"

"Why no, sir." Lynch licked his lips and shuffled his feet around. "Now, I don't say it was apurpose, you mind, but Mr. Buckhorn's riders whooped it up t'other side of the crick where I had the land new seeded. Drove some cows through and trampled it all up and ruint my seeding. I'm not meaning to prod anyone, but I got to pertect myself. You see how it is."

Pa didn't, for a fact. "You wire your side borders on Buckhorn's range first off?"

"Well, no," Joe Lynch said helplessly. "Not yet. You see——"

"I see right enough. You figured to wire off my side first, try me out before you brave Buckhorn." The blood was high in the old man's face, and he was madder than

I'd seen him. "That was your big mistake. No one pushes Jud Tasker. No one!"

He lifted the coiled rope from his pommel and shook it out. He dabbed off a short loop and snaked it over the nearest post. "Your rope!" he snapped at me. My fingers were shaking as I followed up.

We dallied and heeled off to take up the slack. As the horses leaned into it, little mounds of earth broke up around the base of the post. Finally it came free and sagged over.

Quick as a flash Pa turned his horse. Joe Lynch had sidled over by his wagon and was fumbling under the seat. Pa rode against him and the lineback's shoulder smashed Lynch in the chest and bowled him butt over tea kettle in the dust.

Pa reached under the seat and came up with an old Sharps buffalo gun. He opened the breech and pulled out the four inch fifty-caliber shell and tossed the gun back in the wagon.

Pa's eyes were the color of ice. "If you ain't a man, you hadn't better go armed like one."

Joe Lynch crawled to his feet and didn't look up, wiping his hand across his mouth.

"Hear me good. I make you a yellow back-sneaking dog. You are pulling that fence down now, mister, hear?"

"Yes, sir." Lynch said it soft, his shoulders slumped.

"I find it up again, I'll shoot you on sight. Make me out clear, nester?"

"Yes, sir." Lynch's voice came thin, with a quiver to it.

We coiled and slung our ropes. Pa swung off and I followed. He didn't look back, so neither did I. My belly felt a mite snakey. More than once I had got my boy's pride flattened by the weight of Pa's hand, and I thought of the crushed look in Joe Lynch's mild eyes. He was a bent, scrawny one for certain, but he was a man—or had been before he became a lousy nester.

With that I pushed the notion out of mind. As Pa said later on that day, show these damn' hoegrubbers a soft side one time, and they would get mean and snotty.

Next day was Saturday and that meant town day. Pa hitched up the spring wagon and we went in, Ma beside him on the seat and me in the back end hanging my heels over the let-down tailgate.

Pima Flats wasn't much in these days—one dusty street and dirt sidewalks, a general merchandise store, feed company, blacksmith shop, stable, professional building, and a couple of saloons.

The tie rails were already lined with rigs and saddle horses. Pa set our wagon between two others in front of Marsh Whalen's general merchandise store, and then got to the ground and helped Mother down. They hadn't spoke much since the day before. Pa tramped stiff-backed around the wagon and headed for the Shorthorn Saloon across the way to find a rancher crony or two. I skipped along behind Ma, going into Whalen's store.

It was a favored place of mine, old Marsh's. It was cool and smelled of far-off places, of spices and new leather and kerosene. Flocks of women were clucking around between the counters; Ma joined a covey of them. There were some little kids hanging on their mas' skirts, but none near my own age, so I made to ignore the lot, going over to where the stick candy was. Usually old Marsh gave me a free piece if I hung over the counter a spell.

I was eating it up with my eyes and didn't look around

till I heard a man say something to old Marsh. It was Joe Lynch with his wife and the five towheads. Mrs. Lynch was a timid kind of soul with a washed-out look. The kids—two boys and three girls—were all runty for their ages, shy as mice, and they had a scary-eyed look except for the oldest one.

Now with this whole towhead brood standing a yard off, I got up my hackles and put a stare on that oldest Lynch kid. I'd never seen him close before. His name was Marty, and I guess he was my age, but maybe a half a head shorter and mostly bone and skin and tow-colored hair. Me, I was already running to Pa's beef. Pretty soon his eyes, like pale moons in his thin face, dropped away from mine. Which made me rooster my chest out some.

Meantime old Marsh Whalen, a kindly rabbit of a gent, was talking low with the kid's old man. "Don't know as I should stretch your credit one cent more, Mr. Lynch. Folks're already down on me for selling you them bales of barbed wire."

"Sure." Joe Lynch sounded like he was past caring much.

"Allowing folks are dependent on me to freight in their supplies, I can't afford losing a lot of good will."

"Sure. Ain't asking for no more wire, Mr. Whalen. I need to have grub, though. Some more seed, too."

"Well now," said Marsh.

He broke off and some tight lines pinched up his old face. He was looking at the doorway. I faced around and saw Hugh Buckhorn standing there, a squarish big block of a man who looked like he was wedged in his black broadcloth suit. The trousers were stuffed into bench-made Justins and a white Stetson rode his handsome crop of pure white hair. His face looked like it had been chipped from the side of a mountain. He fingered an inch of ash off his palm-held cigar and didn't say anything. Just looked at poor old Marsh.

Off behind him, but in plain sight, stood Bourke Claypool, a long, lean, elegant sort who wore neat range clothes and was no cowhand. There was a black-butted Colt's in a beautifully tooled holster along his thigh. Bourke had a generally bad name, and of course all us kids looked up to him in an inside-out way. Gaming sometimes, we used to bloody noses over whose wooden gun would be Bourke Claypool's. There was Bourke and there was General Custer. You had your pick how you wanted to be killed.

Old Marsh, he swallowed spit a couple times and allowed he couldn't sell Lynch a thing. Sorry. Hugh Buckhorn and his shadow moved out of the doorway and walked on. Joe Lynch stared down at his scuffed thick shoes and didn't say anything.

I saw Ma walk off from the other women, over to Addie Lynch. She said something quiet and nice, and Mrs. Lynch give a timid smile. A few other ladies came over and joined them. The rest sniffed and took on well-I-never expressions.

Joe Lynch got warm under the collar. "Come on."

"I'll stay a little while, please, Joe."

Joe Lynch flung out, "Have it your way," and walked from the store, his steps long and angry. He didn't like his wife taking charity friendship, and I wasn't het on Ma giving it. In those days there was only one brace of pants to a family, and Pa wore 'em. Here was Ma going flat against him, taking up friendly with these nesters. I expect I puffed my crop a bit, because Ma's mouth tightened up.

She looked at the oldest Lynch kid scuffing his barefeet on the planks and said, "Tim, why don't you take Marty and find some of the other boys?"

She flattened my glare with one of her own, and I went out muttering. The Lynch kid tagged along. I got off a ways and turned on him. "Don't want you tagging me, kid."

I stood in front of him and above him and planted my hands on my hips. He looked me over sober and careful. "Why not?"

"Taskers don't have truck with no 'count poor trash."

The kid's pale eyes flared and he tucked his chin. "You better take that back."

"What you gonna do about it?" I put all the sneer in it I could. "Bet you're as yella as your old man."

Right off, I expected he would bluster some. Boys used to brag up to a fight and maybe set a chip on their shoulder and toe a line or two in the dirt. But this runty squirt didn't waste a word. He just lit into me, his skinny arms windmilling.

Next I knew, I was flat on my back with this Lynch runt standing over me and his fists doubled. A thin laugh sounded. I twisted a look around. There was Bourke Claypool, lounging by the tie rail a couple yards away. Bourke's black eyes were dancing, and his grin was mocking and lazy.

"Drag out them spurs, rooster. You ain't letting a chicken-livered hoegrubber stomp you now, are you?"

I crawled up and went after the Lynch kid, swinging wild. He was pretty fast. He stepped off from my first couple swings, then I caught him flush on the jaw and put him down in the dust. I straddled him and pinned his elbows with my knees and began punching his face. Some woman let out a screech. I was crazy mad, and I kept hitting till a big hand clamped around my neck and set me on my feet.

"Lordy, boy," Pa said very quiet. "Lordy, boy. You're half again his size."

Bourke Claypool's thin laugh echoed again. I looked around, breathing hard, seeing the shame in Pa's face, and a kind of protest boiled up in my throat. *What about Lynch, Pa? What about him?*

I left it unsaid. Ma stood in the store doorway, looking a little white around the mouth. Mrs. Lynch was on her knees by Marty and crying and wiping his bloody face on her faded skirt. There and then all the rage was drained out of me, and I stood there with a foolish and belly-down feel.

Joe Lynch came out of the blacksmith shop now and crossed the street at a tired, shuffling run. He shook his wife by the shoulder, asking her the question, and when she answered, he faced around. His eyes targeted me first, but I don't think he really saw me. He looked at Pa then, like he was looking through him, and Pa pulled his glance away.

"If you're through here, Martha," Pa's deep voice was none too steady, "we'll be going home."

There was no talk on the ride back or during the noon meal, nor afterward. There was work to do, but none of us stirred ourselves. I moped in a corner. Pa sat at the table, puffing his pipe like mad. Ma stared at the untouched food on her plate and made no move to clear the table.

Finally, Ma said, very quiet, not looking up, "We should all be very proud of ourselves. Are you proud, Tim?"

"No'm," I muttered.

"Why not ask me, Martha?" Pa didn't sound angry, just tired and a little baffled, like he was trying to study things out.

"Jud." Her voice was very gentle. "Jud, you're the master in this house, and that's as it should be. I can't make your decisions. I should have known that. I tried to push you before, and that was a mistake. I won't make it again."

Pa motioned with his pipe. "Say it anyhow. There's a thing working in me, and I don't know how to put it."

Ma leaned toward him with a kind of glow in her face. "Jud, your self-respect is the root of your life. It has been since I first knew you. And now the root is being torn out, and that isn't right. It's just that you never saw how other people have lives to live too, and a pride that keeps them going. They have a right to that pride."

Pa sighed, long and deep. "Yes, that's it. Martha, I don't know that I can feel the right of anything any more. I used my strength yesterday to smash a weaker man down. Why, yesterday I'd of skinned Tim alive for mauling a lad half his size. Lord! how do you blame a boy for following his Pa?" He puffed hard on his pipe, like he did when downwind of a strong thought, and he said, "Martha, a man can't take back a mistake that bad. But he can grow with it and live better for it."

"Why, Jud, you've said it all yourself!" Ma said, real proud.

I suppose up to that moment Pa was God to me. Seeing him as just a big man, capable of big mistakes, of big regrets, twisted hard in me. Growing up is not a sudden thing, and reaching a foot or so toward manhood in one day can make for some tall hurting. You have been choking down too much in favor of a clay-footed idol; you flounder and you hurt. Still. . . .

Pa was no god, but it took a mighty big man to change the set of his ways when youth was far behind him. I was the lucky one, and I knew it. I ran over to him and he held me tight for a minute, and Ma looked on, not tearful but a little misty.

"Come on." Pa was gruff again. "We got a thing to do, you and me."

The two of us left the house and got our horses. I didn't have to ask, I knew where we was headed.

Around mid-afternoon we came to the Lynch homestead on the east bank of Tie Creek. We stopped up on a rise west of the layout. It didn't take an Injun eye to study out something was wrong. Down along the creek bank a cluster of mounted men was gathered around one of the huge old trees we called an ironwood.

Pa, he socked in steel and boiled down that rise, me a horse's nose behind him.

Mrs. Lynch stood in the door of the shack, her scared towheads grabbing ahold of her skirt. Her face was white as plum blossoms, and she had a wild eye. We went off on past 'em, over to that ironwood.

The horsemen broke apart as we came up, and Joe Lynch was sitting one of his spavined plow horses, wearing a rope jerked up so tight his head was angled sideways and he was fighting for breath. The rope was flung over a big old limb, and a Chainlink hand was tying down the free end.

Pa halted a few yards off and made a motion I was to

rein away from him. I did so, feeling a knot of trouble doubling up in my craw. I was sure there was going to be trouble when Hugh Buckhorn cantered out from the group on his fine special-gaited sorrel. Bourke Claypool edged up too, making it casual. The four Chainlink crewmen, just workaday hands, stayed by the tree. These were times for touching off the mean in a man's soul, and the good, and these fellows were not sure which way they were going. They looked uneasy, even shamefaced.

Hugh Buckhorn crossed his heavy scarred hands on his pommel, his voice a-crackle with authority. "I'm hanging him, Jud. I trust you got no objection?"

Pa said, slow and easy, "That's pendin' you say why."

"Why? An hour ago we caught this damn' cocky sodbuster stringing his wire on my west range."

"Along the boundary of his homestead?" Pa suggested, very dry.

Well, it was that plain. First off Lynch had been timid enough to feel out just us with his wire-stringing. After what happened that morning, he'd found it in him to tackle the big dog, Buckhorn.

Hugh Buckhorn's meaty face was sweating, but it was from the heat. His times hadn't bred the fearing strain, and when they did crop up, they didn't last long. This Buckhorn was of a breed which handled their own problems, shot their own dogs, and it had turned old Hugh hard as flint.

"I ain't bandying that point, Tasker. There's a limit to what a man can take."

"Why, Hugh, I'd say so. Run your cattle through his new-seeded fields, didn't you?"

"Hell fire, man! Don't give me a scripture reading.

Lynch said you made him tear down a length of wire he strung on your side yesterday. Says he's sorry he let you buffalo him, says he's glad to take on the lot of us." Saddle leather creaked to his shifting weight. "I ain't liking this much, but it's the frying pan or the fire. A man takes his choice."

"He does," Pa says softly. "I come to apologize to Joe Lynch."

Bourke Claypool gave a short ugly snicker. "Mr. Tasker, you better make it fast."

"Why bring him back here to string him up? Why make his wife and young 'uns watch it?"

"An object lesson to future nesters. I want this told around. It will head off a lot of future trouble. Now you ride out, dammit, Jud. I want no trouble with you."

You didn't argue it. He was an old man who had outlived two wives and three sons, and the days he'd known had burned out the humanity in him. So Pa half-reined his horse around as if to go. Then his hand, hid to Buckhorn's view, snaked down to the saddle scabbard and tugged out his carbine and brought it up sharp and swift, left forearm bracing the barrel, right hand levering the weapon lightning-fast, then ready to the trigger.

"You ain't hanging Lynch. Tell that hand to cut the rope. Now."

Buckhorn's eyes glittered snake-cold, and I knew how it would be, knew in the split second before he mouthed the flat word, "Bourke!"

Bourke Claypool moved faster than I'd of reckoned a gunman could, straddling leather. The hair-triggered gun blurred from its black sheath. Pa gave his lineback one spur and sent it careening in a half-circle while

Claypool's shot smashed down the hot silence. He scored a clean miss.

Pa reined in the lineback with an iron hand, at the same time bringing the carbine to bear level. It was like an invisible fist hit Bourke Claypool and wiped him off his saddle. He hit the ground and rolled and lit on his back with a sightless stare fixing the sky.

Pa levered the carbine, the sound making my nerves jerk like the shots hadn't. He dead centered the sights on old Huch Buckhorn's broad chest. "Say how it'll be, Hugh. Now, for I won't wait."

Buckhorn's long white hair plumed in the wind; his granite face didn't twitch by a muscle. "You goddamn nester-loving fool," he said, very stony and clear. "I never give a damn what you or any man thought. Cut him loose, Calem."

He spoke true enough; he was a man looking into the hot muzzle of death and knowing it and shaping his action to the size of the stakes. The Buckhorn legend might sit shakier after today, but a dead man would never care. Silently one of the crewmen cut away the rope around Joe Lynch's neck. Another freed the nester's hands. The other two walked to Claypool and lifted his body across his saddle. Mounting, they rode away, tight-bunched.

The near-scrape hadn't touched the crazy and dogged something in Joe Lynch's face as he tramped past us, past his family, into his shack. He come out with the old Sharps gun in his right fist. This, I knew then, was another man, a man grown tall.

"I want to know now and for good, is the trouble done between us?"

"I apologize to you, for me, for my boy." Pa scowled and swallowed with the words, for a prideful man doesn't change. "It's done all right, Joe."

"The fence," Joe Lynch went on, then hesitated. "Say we leave it down for now, see how things go."

Pa nodded and touched his hat to Mrs. Lynch and reined around and away. I started around too, but then reined back. Making my apology was my place, not Pa's.

I looked at Marty Lynch. "You want to come over some time?"

"Maybe."

The kid sounded pretty stiff, and I reckoned he was taking after his old man too. It would take a spell, but I judged he would come. And he did.

AN UNFORGETTABLE SAGA OF THE AMERICAN FRONTIER IN THE TRADITION OF *LONESOME DOVE*.

RED IS THE RIVER
T.V. OLSEN

Winner Of The Golden Spur Award

When Axel Holmgaard discovers his land being flooded by wealthy loggers, his fury explodes. Almost beyond reason, he spends every waking hour trying to wrench justice from the Gannetts. But the Gannetts are equally stubborn and vengeful. They swear a fight to the death.

Adam Gannett would like nothing better than to drive the Holmgaards from the territory. But his unexpected love for their young daughter causes a new turn in the bloody battle.

As the deadly feud rages, Axel and Adam spur their kin on to defeat their enemies. But nothing either man does can stop the love that will save—or destroy—two proud families and everything they believe in.

_3747-5 $4.99 US/$5.99 CAN

Dorchester Publishing Co., Inc.
65 Commerce Road
Stamford, CT 06902

Please add $1.75 for shipping and handling for the first book and $.50 for each book thereafter. NY, NYC, PA and CT residents, please add appropriate sales tax. No cash, stamps, or C.O.D.s. All orders shipped within 6 weeks via postal service book rate. Canadian orders require $2.00 extra postage and must be paid in U.S. dollars through a U.S. banking facility.

Name_____
Address_____
City _____ State_____Zip_____
I have enclosed $_____in payment for the checked book(s).
Payment <u>must</u> accompany all orders.☐ Please send a free catalog.

THERE WAS A SEASON
T.V. OLSEN

Winner Of The Golden Spur Award

A sprawling and magnificent novel, full of the sweeping grandeur and unforgettable beauty of the unconquered American continent—a remarkable story of glorious victories and tragic defeats, of perilous adventures and bloody battles to win the land.

Lt. Jefferson Davis has visions of greatness, but between him and a brilliant future lies the brutal Black Hawk War. In an incredible journey across the frontier, the young officer faces off against enemies known and unknown…tracking a cunning war chief who is making a merciless grab for power…fighting vicious diseases that decimate his troops before Indian arrows can cut them down…and struggling against incredible odds to return to the valiant woman he left behind. Guts, sweat, and grit are all Davis and his soldiers have in their favor. If that isn't enough, they'll wind up little more than dead legends.

_3652-5 $4.99 US/$5.99 CAN

Dorchester Publishing Co., Inc.
65 Commerce Road
Stamford, CT 06902

Please add $1.75 for shipping and handling for the first book and $.50 for each book thereafter. NY, NYC, PA and CT residents, please add appropriate sales tax. No cash, stamps, or C.O.D.s. All orders shipped within 6 weeks via postal service book rate. Canadian orders require $2.00 extra postage and must be paid in U.S. dollars through a U.S. banking facility.

Name_____
Address_____
City _____ State_____ Zip_____
I have enclosed $_____in payment for the checked book(s).
Payment <u>must</u> accompany all orders.☐ Please send a free catalog.

Arrow In The Sun
T. V. Olsen

Bestselling Author Of *Red Is The River*

The wagon train has only two survivors, the young soldier Honus Gant and beautiful, willful Cresta Lee. And they both know that the legendary Cheyenne chieftain Spotted Wolf will not rest until he catches them.

Gant is no one's idea of a hero—he is the first to admit that. He made a mistake joining the cavalry, and he's counting the days until he is a civilian and back east where he belongs. He doesn't want to protect Cresta Lee. He doesn't even like her. In fact, he's come to hate her guts.

The trouble is, Cresta is no ordinary girl. Once she was an Indian captive. Once she was Spotted Wolf's wife. Gant knows what will happen to Cresta if the bloodthirsty warrior captures her again, and he can't let that happen—even if it means risking his life to save her.

__3948-6 $4.50 US/$5.50 CAN

Dorchester Publishing Co., Inc.
65 Commerce Road
Stamford, CT 06902

Please add $1.75 for shipping and handling for the first book and $.50 for each book thereafter. NY, NYC, PA and CT residents, please add appropriate sales tax. No cash, stamps, or C.O.D.s. All orders shipped within 6 weeks via postal service book rate. Canadian orders require $2.00 extra postage and must be paid in U.S. dollars through a U.S. banking facility.

Name_____
Address_____
City _____ State_____ Zip_____
I have enclosed $_____ in payment for the checked book(s).
Payment <u>must</u> accompany all orders.☐ Please send a free catalog.

T.V. OLSEN

Don't miss these double shots of classic Western action!
$7.98 values for only $4.99!
"Plenty of crunching fights and shootings!
Don't pass T.V. Olsen up!"
—*The Roundup*

The Man From Nowhere. Rescued from a watery grave by a rough-hewn ranch family, outlaw Johnny Vano is determined to repay the kindness. But he soon finds out that it's easier to dodge the law than stop a cattle-rustling conspiracy dead in its tracks.

And in the same action-packed volume...

Bitter Grass. Jonathan Trask has survived the loss of his ranch and all the misfortune the world can offer. But when he realizes he's responsible for the one thing that can break him, Trask has to act quickly—or the taste of lead will be the best death he can hope for.

__3728-9 THE MAN FROM NOWHERE/BITTER GRASS (2 books in one) for only $4.99

High Lawless. Bent on avenging his partner's death, Channing finds himself in the middle of a seething range war. He is ready to outgun any man who crosses his sights, but it will take a blazing shootout to settle all the scores.

And in the same exciting volume...

Savage Sierra. The four renegades after Angsman insure that he is going to have trouble staying alive, if the three fools Angsman is leading across the desert don't see to it first. But he knows a man stays dead a long time, and he isn't ready to go to hell yet.

__3524-3 HIGH LAWLESS/SAVAGE SIERRA (2 books in one) for only $4.99

Dorchester Publishing Co., Inc.
65 Commerce Road
Stamford, CT 06902

Please add $1.75 for shipping and handling for the first book and $.50 for each book thereafter. NY, NYC, PA and CT residents, please add appropriate sales tax. No cash, stamps, or C.O.D.s. All orders shipped within 6 weeks via postal service book rate. Canadian orders require $2.00 extra postage and must be paid in U.S. dollars through a U.S. banking facility.

Name_____
Address_____
City _____ State_____ Zip_____
I have enclosed $_____in payment for the checked book(s).
Payment <u>must</u> accompany all orders. ☐ Please send a free catalog.

GLORIETA PASS

GORDON D. SHIRREFFS

Quint Kershaw—legendary mountain man, fighter, and lover—is called from the comforts of the land he loves to battle for the Union under Kit Carson. His mission is to help preserve New Mexico from the Confederate onslaught in a tempestuous time that will test the passions of both men and women.

His sons, David and Fransisco, turn deadly rivals for the love of a shrewd and beautiful woman. His daughter, Guadelupe, yearns deeply for the one man she can never have. And Quint himself once again comes face-to-face with golden-haired Jean Calhoun, the woman he has never gotten out of his mind, now suddenly available and as ravishing as ever.

_3777-7 $4.50 US/$5.50 CAN

Dorchester Publishing Co., Inc.
65 Commerce Road
Stamford, CT 06902

Please add $1.75 for shipping and handling for the first book and $.50 for each book thereafter. NY, NYC, PA and CT residents, please add appropriate sales tax. No cash, stamps, or C.O.D.s. All orders shipped within 6 weeks via postal service book rate. Canadian orders require $2.00 extra postage and must be paid in U.S. dollars through a U.S. banking facility.

Name _____
Address _____
City _____ State _____ Zip _____
I have enclosed $_____ in payment for the checked book(s). Payment <u>must</u> accompany all orders. ☐ Please send a free catalog.

THE MANHUNTER GORDON D. SHIRREFFS

2 ACTION-PACKED WESTERNS IN ONE RIP-ROARIN' VOLUME!

"Written by the hand of a master!"
—*New York Times*

The Apache Hunter. Lee Kershaw is out for the bounty on Yanozha, the ruthless Apache. But the brave is laying his own ambush—and soon Kershaw is being hunted by the deadliest enemy of all.
And in the same action-packed volume....

The Marauders. When Kershaw is hired to track down a shipment of stolen weapons, the trail leads to a bloodthirsty colonel carving his own empire out of Mexico. In his battle against the mad soldier, Kershaw will need all his strength and cunning—or the courage to die like a man.

_3872-2 **(two rip-roaring Westerns in one volume)** $4.99 US/$6.99 CAN

Bowman's Kid. With a silver button as his only clue, Lee Kershaw sets out to track down a boy abducted almost twenty years earlier by the Mescalero Indians. Kershaw has been warned to watch his back, but he hasn't earned his reputation as a gunman for nothing.
And in the same rip-roarin' volume....

Renegade's Trail. Kershaw has never met his match in the Arizona desert—until he is pitted against his ex-partner, the Apache Queho, in the world's most dangerous game: man hunting man.

_3850-1 **(two complete Westerns in one volume)** $4.99 US/$6.99 CAN

Dorchester Publishing Co., Inc.
65 Commerce Road
Stamford, CT 06902

Please add $1.75 for shipping and handling for the first book and $.50 for each book thereafter. NY, NYC, PA and CT residents, please add appropriate sales tax. No cash, stamps, or C.O.D.s. All orders shipped within 6 weeks via postal service book rate. Canadian orders require $2.00 extra postage and must be paid in U.S. dollars through a U.S. banking facility.

Name_____
Address_____
City _____ State_____Zip_____
I have enclosed $_____in payment for the checked book(s).
Payment <u>must</u> accompany all orders.☐ Please send a free catalog.

WILDERNESS GIANT SPECIAL EDITION:

PRAIRIE BLOOD
David Thompson

The epic struggle for survival on America's frontier—in a Giant Special Edition!

While America is still a wild land, tough mountain men like Nathaniel King dare to venture into the majestic Rockies. And though he battles endlessly against savage enemies and hostile elements, his reward is a world unfettered by the corruption that grips the cities back east.

Then Nate's young son disappears, and the life he has struggled to build seems worthless. A desperate search is mounted to save Zach before he falls victim to untold perils. If the rugged pioneers are too late—and Zach hasn't learned the skills he needs to survive—all the freedom on the frontier won't save the boy.

_3679-7 $4.99

Dorchester Publishing Co., Inc.
65 Commerce Road
Stamford, CT 06902

Please add $1.75 for shipping and handling for the first book and $.50 for each book thereafter. NY, NYC, PA and CT residents, please add appropriate sales tax. No cash, stamps, or C.O.D.s. All orders shipped within 6 weeks via postal service book rate. Canadian orders require $2.00 extra postage and must be paid in U.S. dollars through a U.S. banking facility.

Name_____
Address _____
City _____ State_____Zip_____
I have enclosed $_____in payment for the checked book(s).
Payment <u>must</u> accompany all orders.☐ Please send a free catalog.

TWICE THE FRONTIER ACTION AND ADVENTURE IN GIANT SPECIAL EDITIONS!
WILDERNESS GIANT SPECIAL EDITIONS
David Thompson

The Trail West. Far from the teeming streets of civilization, rugged pioneers dare to carve a life out of the savage frontier, but few have a prayer of surviving there. Bravest among the frontiersmen is Nathaniel King—loyal friend, master trapper, and grizzly killer. But when a rich Easterner hires Nate to guide him to the virgin lands west of the Rockies, he finds his life threatened by hostile Indians, greedy backshooters, and renegade settlers. And if Nate fails to defeat those vicious enemies, he'll wind up buried beneath six feet of dirt.
_3938-9 $5.99 US/$7.99 CAN

Ordeal. Back before the poison of civilization corrupts the wilds of the Rocky Mountains, brave mountain men struggle to carve a life from virgin land. When one party of pioneers disappears, Nate King and his mentor Shakespeare McNair are hired to track them down. The perils along the way are unending, but if Shakespeare and Nate survive, they will earn the greatest reward imaginable: the courage to live free.
_3780-7 $4.99 US/$5.99 CAN

Dorchester Publishing Co., Inc.
65 Commerce Road
Stamford, CT 06902

Please add $1.75 for shipping and handling for the first book and $.50 for each book thereafter. NY, NYC, PA and CT residents, please add appropriate sales tax. No cash, stamps, or C.O.D.s. All orders shipped within 6 weeks via postal service book rate. Canadian orders require $2.00 extra postage and must be paid in U.S. dollars through a U.S. banking facility.

Name _____
Address _____
City _____ State _____ Zip _____
I have enclosed $_____ in payment for the checked book(s).
Payment <u>must</u> accompany all orders. ☐ Please send a free catalog.

WILL COOK
Don't miss these double shots of classic Western action!
$7.98 values for only $4.99!
"Cook unwinds a real corker cramjammed with suspense!" —*Oakland Tribune*

Fort Starke. The Arizona Territory is quiet because its fiercest war chief, Diablito, has fled to Mexico. One man is all Diablito wants—the Apache killer, Gentry. And when the bloodthirsty warrior returns, the Indian killer will be the last hope for everyone in Fort Starke.
And in the same action-packed volume...
First Command. Fresh out of West Point, Lt. Jefferson Travis counts on doing everything by the book to keep out of trouble. But in the merciless Kansas Territory, Travis will need more than rules to survive—he'll need guts and strength no book can teach him.

_3590-1 FORT STARKE/FIRST COMMAND (2 books in one) for only $4.99

Badman's Holiday. To the people of Two Pines, Sheriff Lincoln McKeever is just a man with an easygoing smile. They've forgotten about his reputation and the unmarked graves in the cemetery over the hill—and that mistake will cost some of them their lives.
And in the same exciting volume...
The Wind River Kid. Seething with hate and bound for hell, the Wind River Kid makes his worst mistake when he tries to hide in Rindo's Springs. Old Cadmus Rindo owns everyone in the one-horse town—what he doesn't own, he destroys.

_3614-2 BADMAN'S HOLIDAY/THE WIND RIVER KID (2 books in one) for only $4.99

Dorchester Publishing Co., Inc.
65 Commerce Road
Stamford, CT 06902

Please add $1.75 for shipping and handling for the first book and $.50 for each book thereafter. NY, NYC, PA and CT residents, please add appropriate sales tax. No cash, stamps, or C.O.D.s. All orders shipped within 6 weeks via postal service book rate. Canadian orders require $2.00 extra postage and must be paid in U.S. dollars through a U.S. banking facility.

Name_____
Address_____
City _____ State_____ Zip_____
I have enclosed $_____in payment for the checked book(s).
Payment <u>must</u> accompany all orders. ☐ Please send a free catalog.

ATTENTION PREFERRED CUSTOMERS!

SPECIAL TOLL-FREE NUMBER
1-800-481-9191

Call Monday through Friday
**12 noon to 10 p.m.
Eastern Time**
*Get a free catalogue
and order books using your
Visa, MasterCard,
or Discover®*

*Leisure
Books*